THE PROBLEM AT PIHA

Piha is a small beach settlement in New Zealand. Some go there to fish, swim or sunbathe, others to plant cannabis seedlings or to follow 'alternative lifestyles'. In this peaceful setting, nobody expects to be pushed over the sides of the huge Lion Rock, or to be stabbed with a fishing knife. As police invade the district and fear spreads, three elderly clergymen find themselves involved in hunting down a murderer.

FREDA BREAM

◆

THE
PROBLEM
AT PIHA

Complete and Unabridged

LINFORD
Leicester

First published in Great Britain

First Linford Edition
published February 1995

British Library CIP Data

Bream, Freda
    The problem at Piha.—Large print ed.—
Linford mystery library
I. Title II. Series
823 [F]

ISBN 0-7089-7648-4

Published by
F. A. Thorpe (Publishing) Ltd.
Anstey, Leicestershire

Set by Words & Graphics Ltd.
Anstey, Leicestershire
Printed and bound in Great Britain by
T. J. Press (Padstow) Ltd., Padstow, Cornwall

This book is printed on acid-free paper

1

PIHA BEACH lies on the west coast of New Zealand, twenty-six miles distant from Auckland across the Waitakere ranges. Piha is a Maori word meaning 'ripple' but that is a gross understatement for the force of the angry surf which pounds onto the grey-black iron sands of the beach, hurls itself against the volcanic rocks at the base of the cliffs and seeks to sweep away and engulf any fisherman who dares to stand within its reach. In the summer months, when holiday-makers crowd the area, the beach is patrolled by volunteer life guards who place flags on the sand to indicate the limits within which it is relatively safe to enter the water. Those bathers who ignore the warning and attempt to swim outside the flagged area are sometimes rescued by the watching members of the Surf Club. Sometimes, on the other hand, they are not, and thereby win for themselves some brief posthumous publicity in a small corner of the daily newspapers.

Those who do not care to bathe can take their daily exercise by climbing Lion Rock, a solid brown hump of conglomerated stone and sediment which stands alone, about a hundred metres high, in the centre of the beach. No one quite knows how it got there but it is picturesque, photogenic and a source of pride to the few permanent residents of the bay. Its surface is a patchy mixture of turf, meagre scrub and rocky outcrops. The contour of its summit reveals the remains of an early Maori pa. Tourists make a point of climbing the Lion. Indeed, it is the recognised thing to do when you visit Piha Beach. The route up through the centre of the slope facing the shore is comparatively safe for young and old, but if you wish to court danger or impress a friend, you can scale the sides, where projecting portions overhang the rocks below.

These opportunities for adventure, added to such amenities as a Post Office (closed on Tuesdays), a general store, a Takeaway Bar, a stream which sometimes floods, a helicopter pad and — not too far away — a nine-hole golf course, have made Piha Beach a popular marine resort. Holiday homes fringe the curving shore line and dot the surrounding hills.

One afternoon in February of last year, in a small Piha cottage owned by the Christian Education Department of the Anglican Church of New Zealand, and rented out at intervals to clergy on leave, sat three reverend gentlemen, sadly lamenting the grievous fall from grace of a fellow ordained minister, a brother servant of the Church.

The Venerable Alan Freeth, archdeacon in an East Coast district, observed sorrowfully, "I see a marked deterioration in him even since this time last year."

3

George Cumbit, canon emeritus, gravely nodded his balding head. "It's distressing to witness his gradual retrogression. Poor soul. But what can one do?"

"I've remonstrated with him. I've pointed out his failings, but to no avail."

"Yet he needs help."

"Indeed he does, but I fear it's not in my power to administer it. He may even be past redemption."

"No one is beyond hope, Alan. It's wrong to talk like that. You know the chap best, Jabal. Perhaps a word or two from you?"

The Reverend Jabal Jarrett, vicar of the Auckland suburban church of St Bernard's, shook his head. "I've tried. But *he would have none of my counsel. He despised my reproof.*"

"That's scarcely to be wondered at," remarked Alan Freeth drily. "You're no great shakes yourself these days."

"My own performance may not be outstanding," admitted Jabal, "but my advice was sound."

"What was it?"

"To get hold of the pro and arrange for lessons."

"Yes, the only resort left to him now, I fear. In my opinion he tends to transfer his weight too soon."

"I feel it's more a matter of the basic stance and grip."

"No, no," said George Cumbit. "It's his shoulder action that's chiefly at fault."

"I don't agree. If you watch the way he bends his right knee . . . "

"He doesn't lead with his hips."

"His left hand's too loose at the top of his swing. Then on the downstroke . . . "

Alan's theory was interrupted by a heavy knocking at the back door of the cottage. George rose, passed out through the kitchen and in a few seconds returned hastily. "It's Mrs Pearce from next door. There's been an accident and it sounds serious. She's sent for the police and a doctor but she'd like one of us there."

"We'd better all go."

Roma Pearce was waiting for them in obvious agitation. She was a young woman whom they had already met, fair, plumpish and pretty, with a round face which normally wore a pleasant smile. Now it was puckered up in anxiety. "Oh, quick, please come." She led the way.

Lupin Lodge (W. M. Harkin Propr. TV. Priv. Fac. All Con.) was a two-storey wooden building, part of which dated from the turn of the century. Originally the home of a kauri milling contractor, it had changed hands several times as the beach became more populated, had been extended, renovated, modernised, redecorated, by successive owners until it now consisted of two main portions — the old kauri house, where the owner and his family lived, and the attached newer part comprising three single and four double bedrooms, each with private bathroom, television, refrigerator and tea-making facilities. A small flat had also been built onto the other side of the old house, and in this flat lived Roma Pearce, widow, receptionist, dogsbody and everyone's friend.

At the back of the building, beside a garage, was a large shed used for various purposes such as mending furniture, cleaning fish, storing goods and housing friends when the bedrooms were full. It was into this shed that Roma Pearce led the three men. In the middle of the floor lay, face upwards, the inert figure of a man. A knife handle protruded from his chest.

"He's still alive," said Mrs Pearce. "I've just found him. I haven't told the Harkins. I popped into my flat to phone the doctor and the constable . . . " She was trying to keep her voice under control but at this point she stopped, put one hand to her mouth and ran out the door.

The archdeacon was already at the injured man's side. He made the sign of the cross and began, "In the name

7

of God the Father . . . "

The Very Reverend George Cumbit had knelt down and placed a hand on the sweating forehead. "The Lord bless you, my son." Jabal Jarrett bent over, interrupting them both. "Who did this to you?" he demanded. The dying man rolled his eyes towards Jabal. He was obviously fully conscious as he made one final effort to speak. When the words came they were low-pitched but clearly audible. "It was Mad's brother — I mean B . . . " His lower jaw dropped and his eyes closed. He spoke no more.

2

"**W**HAT are you doing here anyway, Jabe?"

It was the morning following the tragedy at Lupin Lodge. Much had taken place since the discovery of the body. A police caravan had been brought from Auckland, installed beside the Harkins' shed and connected to power and telephone wires. An ambulance had arrived and departed, presumably removing the body for examination by the forensic pathologists. There seemed to be policemen everywhere. Jabal had already counted three detectives and four uniformed men. One constable guarded the entrance to the shed, two others roamed the Harkin section to keep sightseers out and occupants in. A fourth appeared to be message boy for he was seen hurrying in and out of the house and the caravan and occasionally using the police car on some errand in the neighbourhood. "Hot pies," pronounced Canon Cumbit knowledgeably, as they watched him drive off once more. "All policemen have a taste for hot pies. I happen to know."

The three clergymen had been briefly questioned the previous evening as to the time they entered the shed and whether they had touched the weapon. Their names and home addresses had been noted and the shoes they had worn into the shed had been confiscated. But no formal statements had yet been demanded of them. Now Detective-Inspector Trevor Chambers was facing his old friend Jabal Jarrett across the kitchen table of Canna Cottage. The other two clergy had been introduced and were seated one each side of Jabal, regarding with interest this grey-headed, keen-eyed officer of the law. The situation was a novel experience for them both.

"I had such a surprise when I saw your name," the Inspector went on. "Why aren't you saving souls in Auckland?"

"My curate's minding the parish," Jabal informed him. "We're attending the annual Anglican Clergy Veterans' Northern District Golf Tourney."

"Good Lord! I didn't know there *was* such a thing. On this crummy little course?"

"It's the first time it's been held here. We use a different course each year but always an easy one, because it's a veterans' event. *With us are the grey-headed and very aged men.* Retired clergy are eligible to compete as well as those still actively employed, and a couple of entrants this year are over ninety. So a nine-hole, fairly flat course such as this one is chosen and we play only nine holes for a game. *As thy days, so shall thy strength be.*"

"Now don't come at that! But I'm glad you're here. A lucky break for me. How long are you staying?"

"Another ten days or so. It's not a simple matter of the winner being the one with the lowest score on the course. We're here to enjoy golf, playing as many games as we can, so the tournament's run on the lines of a tennis or croquet contest, both singles and pairs, open and handicap. It takes over a fortnight to work through the draw."

"And you three were billetted together?"

The archdeacon answered. "No, we arranged it. We're from different regions but we know one another from early days."

Jabal explained. *"We took sweet counsel together and walked unto the house of God in company.* Or, if you prefer it, we attended the same theological college as students."

"I do prefer it," said the Inspector. He told the other two, "Jabal and I were at Auckland University together before he went into the Church and he didn't then have this weird habit of quoting the Bible to all and sundry. He was almost sane in those days. Well, I'm delighted to find you here, Jabe."

"It's good to see you again, Trevor, though I'd have preferred more pleasant circumstances. Have you come over now to take our fingerprints and statements?"

"No, Sergeant Ellis will do that in due course. You three aren't very important to him. You can collect your shoes, by the way, when you want to. Just ask at the caravan. It's a pity you all went into the shed. There's such a mess of footprints. Only yours are distinguishable and we're not interested in you."

"Are we exonerated by the sanctity of our profession?" enquired the archdeacon. "That hardly seems fair."

"Heavens, no" said Chambers. "We have no illusions about that. We pulled in a Methodist parson last month for fraudulent conversion of funds — not to mention the Catholic priest who found a means to tap the power lines

13

and stole electricity, or the Baptist fellow who picked up a bank cheque in the street and cashed it — nearly got away with it too — and that Presbyterian minister who set fire to his derelict church hall to claim insurance and build a new one — mind you, *he* claimed he acted for the good of his flock and maybe he thought he did. Then there was a 'grievous bodily harm' conviction against the rector of the Anglican . . . "

"You need not go on," interrupted Jabal. "You've made your point. Why, with such disillusionments to sour you, are you not interested in us as possible criminals?"

"Because we're concentrating on the occupants of the house next door. It appears that no one else could've done the job. It's established that you weren't on the premises until the Pearce woman came to fetch you. Now *she* could've done it. It's very convenient for a killer to pretend to find the body. Jabal, may I count on some help from you in this wretched business?"

"Mrs Pearce didn't do it and there's no need for help, because . . . "

"Do your friends know about your extra-curricular activities?" The interruption emphasised to Jabal the worry and concern that his Inspector friend was experiencing. Thirty-five years in the police force had failed to harden his attitude to violent death and to its widespread resultant misery.

"What does he get up to?" asked Canon Cumbit. "I thought golf was his only vice."

"He has a peculiar talent for identifying the guilty party in a group of suspects and has been of great assistance to the Auckland police on several occasions. I'm hoping he'll lend a hand in this problem."

"There *is* no problem," said Jabal, but before he could explain the Inspector continued.

"It's an inside job, you see. You know the position of the shed. It's just opposite the back door of the

15

Harkins' house and any stranger going to it would have to pass down the northern side of the house or this side of the Lodge. The path runs between this cottage of yours and the Lodge and no doubt you've seen the three men working on the power lines? The poles are right along the track and the workmen could not have failed to notice anyone passing down it. They swear no one did. There's a garage adjoining the shed but both its doors were securely locked. No one could've been hiding there. Casey Harkin and his brother Bruce were working on their boat and its trailer the other side of the house and they're adamant that no one went that way either. So unless they're lying, it must've been one of the household who committed the offence. It could've been one of seven."

"Not really seven," said Jabal. "The victim . . . "

"I understand Mrs Pearce, the receptionist, fetched the three of you.

Tell me just how that happened, will you, Jabe?"

Jabal forbore to say that he had been earnestly trying to. "We were sitting talking over a cup of coffee about mid-afternoon."

"Three forty-five," contributed George Cumbit. "I'd looked at my watch, so I was able to tell the constable that."

"Mrs Pearce came to the door and told us there'd been an accident. We all went over. The man was lying on the floor of the shed and died a few minutes after we arrived. Mrs Pearce had gone outside the shed and was waiting there."

"Do you think she did it herself?"

"We know she didn't. I'm coming to that. She was very upset, but didn't lose her head. We told her the man was dead and she went into the house to inform the family." Inspector Chambers frowned and shook his head at this point and Jabal gathered it had not been correct procedure. He went on, "William Harkin came out. The

17

local constable and the doctor arrived shortly afterwards. When the doctor had examined the body the constable asked him to phone the Auckland CIB while he guarded the entrance to the shed."

"A good man, that," commented the Inspector. "Some local boys can really mess matters up for us, but this fellow did everything according to the book. I'll let it be known in the right quarters."

"After he'd taken our names and home addresses . . . "

"*And* our shoes," murmured George, looking ruefully down at his slippered feet. "I only had that pair besides my golf brogues."

" . . . he told us we could leave. It didn't appear that we could help in any way. Mrs Pearce didn't want us, either. She thanked us for coming, assured us we could be of no further assistance and then . . . "

"More or less kicked us off the property," finished Alan Freeth.

"Well, she *would* if she'd killed

the poor fellow. You'd served your purpose."

"We felt one of us should stay," said the archdeacon, "but it was clear that she didn't want us to and William Harkin just shook his head when we asked him. He seemed dazed with the shock, poor man."

"So you were actually present when the man died?"

"Yes," said Jabal. "He was conscious just long enough to tell us who stabbed him."

"What? He *told* you? Why didn't you say so? Who was it?"

"He said, 'It was Mad's brother. I mean . . . ' Then he started to give the name. I think it began with a B." Jabal looked enquiringly at the others.

"I had the impression it was a B," said Alan. "But I suppose it could have been a P."

"It was a B," affirmed George.

"Are you sure about the rest of what he said?" asked the Inspector.

"Quite," Jabal assured him. "It was

perfectly clear. He spoke with an effort but the words weren't slurred or indistinct. The three of us heard him."

"And the woman who took you over? Mrs Pearce?"

"She was distressed and had gone outside. She could not have heard."

"Hm. 'Mad's brother'. That'll be Madeleine Harkin. You know the set-up, I suppose? Lupin Lodge is owned by the Harkin family. Old man Harkin and his wife died some years ago and the eldest son William carried on the business with the help of his young sister Madeleine. William's married but his wife is at present visiting her parents in Christchurch. There are two other sons, both staying at the place for the summer holidays. So there are three brothers Bruce, Casey and William. Bruce is only a schoolboy, seventeen years old, just finished his last year at Auckland Grammar and enrolled to start University study in March. Bruce — there's a B, and I imagine William

Harkin is called Bill."

"I've not heard him called that," said Jabal. "It's always been Will, Willie or William, but Bill may well be a family name for him. We've been here less than a week and although we've met them all we haven't seen much of them."

"You're sure about the B or P? Can we rule out Casey?"

"It was definitely a plosive sound. The lips would've been parted for a C."

"Had you met the victim, Graham Cowan?"

"Yes. He was a Lodge guest but apparently a friend of the Harkin family because Will introduced him to us. But we hadn't spoken to him since."

"You say the Pearce woman fetched William Harkin while you were still there. What was his reaction?"

"Shocked. If he did the job himself he acted well. Of course he may have rehearsed before we arrived."

Alan protested. "You're too cynical,

Jabal. I'm convinced that Will Harkin was genuinely surprised and upset. And I've never heard anyone call him Bill."

"Then it looks like the boy, Bruce," said the Inspector.

"A teenager?" Alan raised his eyebrows. "Boys that age don't take to murder, do they?"

"Unfortunately yes, they do," said Chambers. "Usually in an emotional fit."

"And could you arrest this lad just on the dying statement of the victim?"

"No, but if there were corroborating factors and he was charged, it could secure a conviction because the declaration of a dying man is one case in which hearsay evidence is admissible in court. It could be damning in this case, where three reputable clergymen would testify."

"You were protesting a few minutes ago that clergymen are not necessarily reputable."

"You're reputable when we want you to be. Your evidence would be of the utmost importance, especially as this fellow was struck from in front and therefore must've seen his assailant. But are you sure that's what he was telling you? 'It was Mad's brother' might mean something else, like 'It was Mad's brother who asked me to come into the shed and fetch a spanner' or 'It was on account of Mad's brother . . . '"

"No," said Jabal firmly. "I asked 'Who did this to you?' He was fully conscious. He understood the question and he answered it."

"Then why didn't he simply say 'It was Bruce' or 'It was Bill' or whatever?"

"Perhaps because we were comparative strangers to him. As I told you, we'd been briefly introduced and that's all. 'Bill' or 'Bruce' might be anyone to us, so he was being more explicit. It's also evident that he regarded his killer in that light — as a brother of Madeleine Harkin rather than in any other capacity. He was going to be more specific but lost power of speech before he could pronounce the actual name. Who was he, Trevor? What do you know about him?"

"Not much yet. He was one of the paying guests in the Lodge, booked in 16th December, home address in Remuera, unmarried, lived alone. A friend of Madeleine Harkin's fiancé, that is . . . " Trevor consulted his notes. " . . . Bradley Sayer, and because of that he was frequently in the Harkins' residential part of the building and knew all the family well. At least, that's the story so far. I've not yet read every report. All the household have had one interview but there's still much to be learned."

"Any question of alcohol?" asked Jabal.

"No. Most quarrels arise from drink or drugs but I don't think either was a factor in this case. All were sober when we arrived."

The canon spoke up. "Bradley — that's another B."

"Yes, but it means nothing. Cowan had been here since before Christmas. He wouldn't confuse Sayer with one of Madeleine's brothers."

"Could the 'Mad' refer to anyone else?"

The Inspector again consulted his notes, then said, "Not among those who could've stabbed Cowan. There's no other name like it and she's the only one of the group with brothers here."

"And they commonly refer to her as 'Mad'," added Jabal. "I imagine that abbreviation would appeal to unfeeling brothers when they were small and it stuck. Are you going to tell the family what Cowan said?"

"I don't think so," said Trevor. "At any rate, not at this stage, and I'd be glad if you three would keep it to yourselves. There's no point in warning the murderer that his identity is known."

Alan asked, "Could the poor man have mistaken the identity of a person who came at him head-on?"

"It's possible, I suppose. An overcoat, hat, glasses, some form of disguise. But I doubt it. The shed has plenty of windows and the light is good. Besides, this appears to have been a spur of the moment crime. Disguise implies planning beforehand. But we can't say it didn't happen. The case isn't as simple as you appear to think, Jabal. Even if we know the killer we have to establish motive and opportunity and gather evidence to submit to a jury. We've taken only preliminary statements as yet. We'll have to question each one of the guests in the Lodge too, although it seems they're in the clear. They might know something or have seen something. There's an awful lot of work to be done, in spite of what you've told me. Every member of the household will have to be thoroughly investigated, each of the seven who *could* have stabbed Cowan. I would like your help, Jabal."

"The Wanganui computer will give

you most of their past history and your men will soon squeeze the rest out of them. Poor wretches. I think you're bringing unnecessary complications into a very straightforward case. But who are these seven?"

"The Harkins — William, Madeleine, Casey and Bruce. Roma Pearce, the receptionist. She was widowed four years ago and since then has worked here, living in a flat attached to the old house. Then Bradley Sayer, who is engaged to Madeleine, and his mother, Mrs Irma Sayer, both invited for the summer holidays. That's the lot. Madeleine and Bruce Harkin are half-sister and half-brother to William and Casey, who are sons of old Harkin's first wife. They are considerably older than Madeleine and Bruce."

"So Bruce is the only real brother?" asked Alan. "That brings your suspects down to one, doesn't it?"

"I doubt it," said Trevor. "When you've just been stabbed in the chest you're hardly likely to be so precise as to

PAP2
27

say 'Mad's half-brother'. Besides, they appear to be a closely-knit family and probably regard themselves as simple brothers and sister. Still, you'll soon find out their attitude concerning that, Jabe."

"I've told you . . . "

The Inspector went on hurriedly, "Bruce makes his home here but has been boarding at the Auckland Grammar hostel in term time. Casey is unmarried, owns a part share in a garage in Auckland and lives in premises over it. Doing very well, I gather. Takes a long holiday each summer, comes over here and according to William Harkin works like a slave for his keep. You say you've met them all. How does Casey strike you."

He looked at the three of them in turn. It was Alan who answered. "We like all the family. Casey's the hairy one — enormous beard and whiskers that make him look like a cross between a gorilla and an Old Testament patriarch. Good sportsman, keen surfer, takes a turn now and then as lifeguard in the Surf Club — the girl says he's been involved in more than one rescue. She's proud of him."

"Yes, a likeable type," agreed George. "Bluff and hearty and friendly."

The Inspector continued, "I interviewed William Harkin myself. He spoke well of his sister and brothers. He says they all pitch in during the summer rush, all pull their weight, and that means a lot to him right now, while his wife's away. A cleaning woman comes in each morning to do the guest rooms, but they see to everything else themselves, with the aid of Roma Pearce, the paid assistant. She seems a decent type, too. Handles all bookings, keeps the keys in her flat, supervises laundry and cleaning and generally makes herself useful. Takes her meals with the family and according to Harkin is regarded more as a close friend than a servant."

Habit made Jabal ask, "Where did the knife come from?"

"It was one kept in the shed, used mainly for cleaning and scaling fish and was sharpened regularly, Harkin says. It looks as though the crime was unpremeditated because anyone with murder in mind would have brought his own weapon. Besides, it's not usual to approach your victim from the front if you plan to kill him. I'd say someone picked up the knife and stabbed in a sudden rage. Our surgeon said it must've been done on the spot and shortly before Roma Pearce went in and found him."

"Do you know what he was doing in the shed?"

"Harkin thinks he must've gone in to borrow or return a tool, or simply to wash his hands. He'd been doing a small job on his car. There's no parking at the Lodge, but the public car park is very close. The shed's left open all the time, there's a sink, soap and towel in it, and it would be easier for Cowan to go in there to wash the grease off his hands rather than up to his room in the Lodge. He'd been invited to use the shed, and the tools in it, any time he wanted to. William Harkin appears to be a very easy-going, friendly chap."

"Why did Mrs Pearce go in?"

"She states that she'd gone in with some old newspapers to store away. An untidy pile of them on the floor near the door bears out that story. She says she just threw them down and rushed over to Cowan."

"Such a shock for the poor girl," murmured George Cumbit.

"Where were the Harkin brothers at the time?" asked Jabal.

"Casey and Bruce were working on the boat round the northern side of the house. Each admits he went inside once or twice but they were on no occasion both away at the same time. Well, that's their story. They're very vague as to times — suspiciously vague."

"Time doesn't matter much at the beach," said Alan. "We only look at the clock ourselves when we have a golf appointment to think about. It's because we were checking up on how much time we had before our next match that we happened to know when it was that Mrs Pearce called."

"Hm. I still consider it suspicious that they had no idea whatever. As for William Harkin, he was replacing a rusted window fastening in the dining room — so he *says* — and having a bit of difficulty in removing the old one. Went out to the shed more than once for a tool. Claims Cowan was not there on any occasion. He had the best opportunity, I'd say. The others . . . "

"It doesn't matter about the others," protested Jabal.

"The others," went on Trevor obstinately, "were also in the house. Mrs Sayer was in the kitchen most of the afternoon, cleaning shelves and tidying up, Bradley Sayer was watching the cricket Test on television with Madeleine in the living room, but Madeleine doesn't share his interest in cricket and left the room several times. Roma Pearce was moving about, answering the telephone, arranging flowers, going into her flat, which opens off the kitchen, to look up bookings and once to fetch a duplicate key which she took over to the Lodge. Moving about all the afternoon. She'd have had a good chance to nip into the shed and stab the chap without being seen. In fact, any of them could've gone out of the house and into the shed without being seen by the others. You know the plan of these old villas, with a central passage and the rooms opening off it. Stairs by the front door but no one was on the upper floor. Just bedrooms and bathroom there. No one person can give another an alibi, not even the two men working on the boat, but of course they all claim that none of them would dream of attacking Cowan and that it must've been a stranger. Sticking together. Won't face facts. Well, that's the gist of it. Now what about it, Jabe? I accept your statement that it was one of the brothers, but I don't think we can rule out William. All Williams are Bill to somebody. Whichever one it was, we still need proof. We'll do all the formal questioning and research but you can chat with the family, find out which of the two did it and what his motive was. He may even tell you. People are inclined to confide in you."

"If either of them told me in my capacity as priest, I could not pass it on to you."

"But you usually arrive at the truth before anyone confesses. Come on, it's not like you to turn down a problem."

"There is no problem, except for motive, and your men will soon ferret that out. The dying man meant what he said and he spoke clearly. It's a simple case. You have only two suspects, only two possibles. I suggest you arrest the one with the better-sounding alibi. *I'm* going to play golf."

3

GOLF is one of the most powerful antidotes known to man against the painful twinges of a conscience. With the prospect of a handicap doubles that afternoon, Jabal had no intention of involving himself in the affair next door. He was very sorry for the Harkin family, even for the one who had lost his temper and killed. If an opportunity arose to offer them comfort or practical help, he would certainly take it. But his detective friend was not in need of help. Trevor Chambers was an able, intelligent, well-experienced police officer, backed up by a competent team of assistants, and with only two starters in the field, his task was simple. Whereas the mastery of Jabal's five iron was demanding his urgent attention. His chip shots yesterday had not only been misjudged as to distance, either falling short of the green or over-running it altogether, but had shown a tendency to travel south-south-east when he aimed south-west. He knew what it was — sloppy wrist action and standing too far from the ball. He should really change to the reverse overlap grip for those shots, as George had suggested. George was having trouble with his woods, but then, as Jabal and Alan had told him, he should not insist on using them on the fairway instead of an iron. As well as landing him in the rough, the habit was ruining his drive from the tee.

Alan had a match scheduled for midday and was to be picked up shortly before then by his partner, but Jabal and George intended to put in some practice before the afternoon's play. It was half-past ten. Trevor Chambers had left them. Alan was making coffee, Jabal and George were discussing the relative merits of the paddock behind the post office, the empty section up the road and the unoccupied portion of the public car park, when William Harkin called.

William was a dark-haired man of medium height, stocky, with strong shoulders, a square face, weatherbeaten skin and clear blue eyes under heavy brows. His manner was open and friendly. "I wanted to thank you for coming over yesterday. Roma says she hesitated to fetch any of the family because it would've been such a shock. She was dreadfully upset herself, poor girl, and I suppose it's natural for some people to turn to the clergy at a time like that. A nasty experience for her."

"A nasty experience for you all," said Alan. "I'm brewing coffee. Will you have a cup with us?"

"Thank you, yes, I'd like to." Will sat down. "It's a rotten business all right. I'm sorry you got mixed up in it. It's sort of rocked the whole bay. Folks don't know what to say or do. Some come and ask questions, once they get past the police. Others turn and scuttle away if they see us on the beach. One dear old soul brought over a cream sponge. It was her way of expressing sympathy."

"I suppose you're well-known to everyone in the bay?"

"To the permanents, yes. We've been here for years. And many of the bach-owners at least know us by name. Everyone seems to be as puzzled and shocked as we are ourselves. And what a blow for Cowan's family! They'll have been told by now. The police were going to do it. My wife, too — it's spoiled her holiday. I phoned through to her to tell her about it before she could read it in the papers. She wants to get the next plane home. I hope she doesn't. I tried to persuade her not to. She's well out of it. But a thing like this affects so many people." Will was speaking in a matter-of-fact tone, but a slight jerkiness in his voice could not be controlled.

Alan nodded his head sympathetically. "Are the guests in the Lodge checking out?"

"I guess they all will when the police let them go. They have to stay put until statements are taken and some of them are getting really snaky over it. They come and protest to us but we can't do anything, except try to soothe them down and tell them it won't be long. It won't either, because the police don't suspect any of them. They think it's one of us. Someone in the house. Inspector Chambers actually said so. That's the worst feature of the whole beastly business. One of us!"

"Do you agree?" asked Jabal.

There was a long pause before Will said, "I can't believe it, yet I don't see how anyone else could've got into the shed without being seen. Casey and Bruce were on one side of the building. You know where Roma's flat juts out? That doesn't leave much room between the house and the fence. The linesmen were working on the other side. As for the back, we put up that high-wire netting fence to keep the Robertsons' goat out and now their thorny bougainvillea has grown tangled all through it. No one could come that way. Can people stab themselves?"

"They can," said Jabal. "It was a popular method of suicide among the ancient Romans and Shakespeare was fond of making his characters despatch themselves that way. But it hasn't often been done since the invention of firearms and the improved access to drugs. It's a silly way to choose to kill oneself, a painful experience if it doesn't succeed. The post-mortem will probably indicate whether the wound could have been self-inflicted. But I don't think you can really hope for a verdict of suicide."

"No, I suppose not."

"If you accept the fact that one of your household did it, which one would you consider most likely?"

There was another long pause. The three clergy were staring at Will, with what he assumed was sympathy and attention. In fact, they were all considering the chances of his being

40

the murderer and trying to read his guilt or innocence from his expression and his words. Either he or his brother Bruce had stabbed a man to death. Was he called Bill? Was his distress assumed, an act put on to deceive them? All three felt pity mixed with their suspicions.

At last he passed a hand over his forehead and spoke again. "Look, it's like a nightmare. Mad and Bruce and Casey are my own sister and brothers. I grew up with them. I *know* them and I just can't imagine any of them wanting to kill a man. Yet . . . " He paused again and then said slowly, "We have to be realistic about this. We can't put our heads in the sand. You never know what a person can be driven to do. I can't swear none of them did it. As for the others — Bradley? Mrs Sayer? Why ever *would* they? Roma? She's been with us nearly four years now and we consider ourselves jolly lucky to have her. She's a thoroughly honest, decent girl and gets on well with everyone. She and Mad are good friends. Of course I

41

don't know everything that goes on. I have my work to do — maintenance of the property and keeping the books, as well as involvement in some local organisations, the Community Centre and the Ratepayers' and Residents' Association and so on. And I do the Surf Club accounts for them. I'm kept busy."

"Did you know Graham Cowan well?"

"No. It's the first time he's come. He arrived about a week before Christmas and discovered Brad was here. They knew each other but had lost touch."

"Why did he come?"

"Just for a few weeks' surfing, I reckon. He brought his own board. The championship events are held here next month and I think he intended to stay for that."

"That's a long holiday."

"He could afford it. He was well-heeled. And we're only an hour's run from Auckland. He could go back to see to any business. That's what Bradley and Casey do. They've both been here since the middle of December. Casey has a good crew working for him and they look after his garage. Brad's a chemist, in with two other guys who both prefer their holidays in winter to travel overseas. His shop's doing very well and they can all afford long breaks."

"What did Cowan do for a living?"

"I'm not sure. I think he had private means and from what he said he was tied up with one or two importing concerns. I don't know any details. He didn't talk much about his work."

"What was your impression of him?"

"He was all right. A bit too keen on Madeleine. Fell for her straight off. He knew she was engaged, he was a so called friend of Bradley, and in my opinion he should have remembered both those facts a little better than he did. She didn't reciprocate. She didn't even like him. She made that clear, so you needn't think Bradley had any need to be jealous and eliminate competition. He wouldn't kill Graham just because he was making passes at his fiancée. Why would *anyone* kill Graham if it comes to that? Yet someone did. The whole thing's crazy, like a ghastly dream."

Canon Cumbit said, "It must be dreadful for you, Mr Harkin. Would you like more coffee?"

"Thank you, yes. But call me Will. No need to be formal at Piha."

"I quite agree," said Alan. "I'm Alan, these are Jabal and George." He gestured with his coffee spoon.

"Are you also known as Bill?" asked Jabal.

"Call me that by all means, if you want to."

"No, no. It just occurred to me that it's the more common abbreviation for William and I wondered if that was a name by which you're known."

Will Harkin looked a little puzzled. "The family never call me Bill. A Lodge guest has sometimes, when he wants to appear matey because he's broken a cup or torn a sheet. And one or two fellows in the Surf Club do."

"Did Graham Cowan call you Bill? I have a reason for asking," added Jabal and hoped he would not be asked what it was.

"Graham? No, I was Will to him." Harkin continued to look puzzled but did not pursue the matter. He said, "Everyone is sort of dazed, as if they can't believe it really happened."

"How is your young brother Bruce reacting?"

"Same as the rest of us. He doesn't say much, but I think he's feeling a bit guilty."

"Guilty?" Three pairs of eyes fastened on William's face.

"Yes, for wishing Graham out of the way. Bruce didn't like Graham much. He resented the attentions he was paying Mad, making a nuisance of himself to her. Bruce and Mad have always been close and Bruce almost hero-worships Bradley. He thought Graham was horning in and might spoil things between Bradley and Mad, so he sometimes said he wished Graham would get the hell out of it. There could be a bit more to it. I had the impression there'd been some disagreement between them. I heard them at loggerheads more than once."

Jabal asked directly, "Will, could Bruce have stabbed Cowan?"

Will did not answer at once. Then he sighed and said, "I've been asking myself that all night. Bruce wouldn't stab anyone if he had time to think about it. I'm quite sure of that. I'd stake my life on it. But if he'd been goaded, suddenly angered on someone else's behalf — say Madeleine's — I can't swear he wouldn't hit out. All the Harkins are quick-tempered. I'm told I'm the most placid of us all but even I can feel an overpowering rage at times. Once when a man on the beach was beating a dog I really lost my cool. I saw red. I wanted to knock his head off, mash him to bits, I was so furious."

"And did you?"

"Not quite. I punched him on the jaw and got myself into trouble for it. 'Assault with intent to injure' reduced to 'Common assault'. I could've got a year's jail. As it was I was threatened with periodic detention but got off with a hundred dollars fine and costs and a severe warning that the sentence wouldn't be so light next time. Oh, I say! That'll be on police records, won't it?"

"They won't arrest you on that account. Do you feel that Bruce reacts the same way if he's pushed?"

"He did as a small kid. I haven't seen him lose his temper lately but I know he hasn't changed. He got into a scrap at school last year, just before the May holidays. Came home with a real shiner. I didn't ask questions. That sort of thing's not uncommon in schoolboys. But I've thought and thought and I always come up with the answer that Bruce couldn't have done anything as violent as this, that he wouldn't kill, even in a rage."

"What about Casey?"

"He's got the worst temper of us all." Will gave a slight smile. "I could tell you some tales about that. His boiling point's very low and it doesn't take much to drive him to action. But that's just it. He wouldn't wait until he was so mad that he was ready to stick a knife in someone. If Cowan got his goat Casey'd let fly with his fist, or else take him by the scruff of the neck and toss him out the door. He wouldn't *kill*."

"Then who did, in your opinion?"

"That's another question I asked myself all night. Look, do you mind if we don't talk about it any more just now? I'm still confused myself and I can't even think clearly. Casey and I are taking the boat out tomorrow if the sea's not too rough and if the police don't forbid it. They might suspect us of trying to escape one thousand miles to Australia in a dinghy. I don't think we'll ask permission in case they say no. There's a few small repairs to do on the boat — it gets a bashing in this surf — and a bit of re-painting, but it should be ready by nine and the tide'll be right for launching it then. Would any of you care to come with us for a spot of fishing? We can take two of you and we have spare lines."

"We're all playing matches tomorrow, thank you," said Alan, "but I'd like to come over and see your boat some time if I may?"

"Any time. Well, good luck in your golf matches. I envy you. Golf used to be my weakness too, but I haven't played for months. No time these days." Will rose. "Thank you for the coffee, and more for your sympathy and letting me chatter about it. It really does help to know someone understands."

The archdeacon showed him out. On his return he regarded Jabal severely. "That poor man! Shouldn't you do as the Inspector asked and look into the matter?"

"That 'poor man' may have stabbed one of his house guests yesterday."

"I know that, but I still feel sorry for him. If he stabbed Cowan, it must've been in a fit of temper, the sort that made him punch the man who was beating the dog. But I don't think he did it. It must have been the other one, Bruce."

George said, "He thanked us for our sympathy and understanding. That made me feel a hypocrite, because I kept wondering if he was going to confess that he was the killer. I really think you ought to help, Jabal."

"There's no point in my taking a hand. You heard the dying man. Could he, could he *possibly*, have meant anything other than what he said?"

"No," admitted Alan. "What he said was clear enough. But surely you could speed things up by investigating the motive. This man Will seems such a thoroughly decent type."

"Murderers often do. He was ready enough to tell us how bad-tempered his brothers are."

"That just shows his open, honest nature."

"Or his desire to put the blame on them. But since he's not known as Bill, I suppose it was the younger one, Bruce."

"A seventeen-year-old?" asked Alan. "There's plenty of violence in my district, gang fights and so on, but serious injuries have been inflicted only by an older age group, those over twenty at least. Do you come across any killers as young as Bruce in these criminal hunts you indulge in between sermons?"

"Certainly. Seventeen is a particularly sensitive and bewildering age, prone to excesses of emotion. I don't think this was a premeditated murder. Few murders are, fortunately. Most are the result of domestic strife and committed in a brief moment of uncontrollable rage, usually induced by alcohol abuse. Drink, drugs, unemployment, strikes, all the frustrations and uncertainties and fears of the present day, are the main causes of the prevalent spate of violence. The killer nearly always experiences an instant remorse which remains with him all his life. He seldom kills again. A young person can turn on a fellow gang member, strike out against a parent trying to impose discipline, and then regret it for the rest of his days. So one can feel sympathy with the killer as well as the victim. At Bruce's age feelings are intense and emotions magnified. A fit of jealousy, indignation, anger, desire to protect his sister, could have caused him to lose control. He may even now be in the throes of the most miserable remorse and self-condemnation. But unless I can help him, I see no reason to interfere."

"All your Inspector friend asked you to do was talk to the household and use your gifts to clarify motive and to get the facts straight, which would cut short the suffering of all concerned."

"The police have every facility for

investigation into all the household's private affairs and past history. It's not a job for anyone else."

"But the Inspector said you often helped the police."

"I've been involved in a few cases, yes, but in a different type of homicide. Cold-blooded, calculated murder is a terrible thing. One who can plan, and then carry out, the deliberate taking of another's life is a menace to society and there's an urgent need to identify and apprehend him as soon as possible. He needs treatment, but more than that, others need to be protected from him. His is a warped, sick, corrupt mind and having killed once he may kill again. The chances are that he will. Each successive killing becomes easier than the last and he can come to regard murder as an automatic means of self-protection or self-promotion. But if young Bruce killed Cowan, it was in a sudden fit of fury and there's little risk that he'll attack anyone else. You heard Will say that all the Harkins have hot tempers. The police will soon find out the nature of Bruce's. Piha residents will be questioned and accounts of previous incidents may be given. His headmaster will be consulted, and his opinion sought on the lengths to which Bruce would go. Moreover, Trevor is a clever man and a shrewd judge of character, well trained in questioning suspects. He'll soon trap the boy. Bruce will confess and the case will be over."

"In time, perhaps," said Alan. "You could hurry matters along and the sooner the affair's cleaned up the better for the whole family, including the killer."

"That's perfectly true," said George. "Don't you feel you owe it to the Harkins? They've been good to us. Bringing us a bottle of fresh milk the day we arrived, for instance, when they didn't even know us."

"They knew our calling," said Jabal, "and to whom this cottage belongs. There's a widespread belief that assistance to the clergy will bleach the stains from one's own soul."

"Assistance to *anyone* surely goes a little way towards it," reproved George.

"And we still had to mix up that dried powdered milk we'd brought."

"Only because you gave the fresh to the cat who walked in."

"Oh yes, Clara," said Jabal. "I'd forgotten that. She looked so pathetic I thought she was an abandoned stray. Deceitful female."

"And what about those hot scones the girl Madeleine brought over the next morning? I don't think she was worrying about her grubby soul. It was pure kindness."

"You're unduly influenced, George, because of your weakness for date scones. *A gift blindeth the wise and perverteth the words of the righteous.*"

"They were good scones," admitted George. "I hope she brings us some more. But the Harkins have helped in other ways, too. Like Casey easing that window for us, and Will unblocking the sink. Don't we owe them something for that? Woe unto him that useth his neighbour's services without wages and giveth him not for his work."

Jabal laughed. "All right, point taken. But I really can't help and there's no point in trying to. If I talked to the boy and he confessed, I couldn't reveal the fact, so it would be no help to Trevor. The youngster may have left his fingerprints on the knife. I hope for his sake that he did. Now come on, George. Get your driver and your practice balls. We're wasting time."

4

"JABAL, come and have a look at the Harkins' boat. They're just going to load it onto the trailer, I think. The sea must be calm enough for them to take it out this morning."

"Alan, you do not deceive me. You've put too much credence in Trevor Chambers' remarks about my ability to detect. You aim to entice me over to the Harkins' while a group is gathered round the boat, in the expectation that I shall ask a few cryptic questions and then announce that the storekeeper's second assistant is a long-lost brother to the Harkins, his real name is Bernard, Brian or Benjamin, and he must be arrested at once."

"It's possible that I did have some such idea. Why not?"

"I tell you that the simplest explanation

of a problem is nearly always the correct one, and the person most likely to have committed a crime is usually the one who did. You can't make a complicated problem out of this Harkin case. It was sudden, it was simple, and the victim himself told us who did it. But I'll come and look at the boat. You, too, George? It may stop you brooding over your ghastly performance yesterday afternoon."

"I don't consider it ghastly. Nine holes in fifty-four is one of my better efforts. But I shan't come with you. I have a couple of shirts to wash. It's not as though we could help the Harkins, or even say anything useful. I wish we could. They must be having a wretched time, poor souls. Was your Inspector friend at their throats all yesterday?"

"I don't know and I shan't ask. We'll talk about dinghies and tides and outboard motors."

Alan and Jabal strolled down the track beside the cottage and round the front of the Lodge. It was a fine, clear morning, with as yet, no sea breeze. The yellow lupins which gave the Lodge its name were glowing in the bright sunlight and vivid blue convolvulus twined through the clumps of tussock grass. Several bathers were already in the water and two members of the Surf Club were adjusting the position of the marker flags. It looked a typical, peaceful holiday scene.

"Listen to the thumping of those waves," commented Alan. "How can they get a boat to the other side of that surf?"

"If anyone can, it will be Casey Harkin. He's a powerful giant. I'm told there are only about three times a year when most boat owners can put out. But not the Harkin brothers. They go when they choose to. Is that young Bruce climbing the Lion?"

A few people could be seen plodding up the centre track of the Rock, but one other was rapidly scaling the right-hand side, surefooted, lithe, pulling himself over the projecting shelves with what appeared to be little effort.

"Yes, that's Bruce. His daily morning exercise, I believe, after a dip in the sea. They seem to be an athletic family."

There were three persons standing by the boat while Clara, the cat, sat idly watching from a few yards away. It was she who first saw and greeted Alan and Jabal. She recognised them, trotted up, rubbed herself against their legs, as well-educated cats are wont to do, and communicated to them loudly, as well-educated cats do, that she was a neglected waif, abandoned by the world, had not eaten for a week, was in desperate need of sustenance and if they happened to have a piece of fresh beef steak in their pocket, she'd be greatly obliged if they'd hand it over forthwith. Then she accompanied them over to the boat.

Casey Harkin gave a friendly wave as he saw them approach. He was a large man, bearded, with thick dark hair and whiskers, and blue eyes. Madeleine, standing beside him, looked frail by contrast. She had the same bright blue eyes as her brother but a fairer skin and light brown hair. Bradley Sayer was cleaning a paint brush on the grass. Both men wore bathing trunks, woollen pullovers and canvas shoes.

"Is it ready to use?" asked Alan.

"More than ready," Casey told him. "We finished repairs yesterday and the rest of the painting this morning. We're fiddling about with it mostly as an excuse to get out of the house."

"Police?" asked Alan sympathetically.

"The police are all right. They stick to their caravan most of the time. It's the blasted reporters. The constables keep them out of the section but they can't stop them phoning and if we're inside we feel obliged to answer the phone in case it's a message for a Lodge guest. But it's nearly always a reporter asking silly questions and fishing for emotional comments. You have to be polite to the blighters or else they'll print lies about you in revenge. So we've walked out and left it to poor Roma. She says she doesn't mind. She's worked up a few formulas to trot out. And Will's there. He had a fit of conscience and we couldn't persuade him to come with us. So he can help her with anything sticky."

"Cheer up," said Bradley Sayer. "You'll be free to ignore the phone soon because the guests are all checking out as soon as they're cleared by the police. There'll be none left in a day or two."

"And that will be the end of Will's business."

"No, memories are short. The Lodge'll be just as popular next season." Bradley was a pleasant-looking, pleasant-voiced young man but the tenseness in his tone belied the cheerfulness of his remarks. Jabal noticed that he kept glancing at Madeleine with a look of concern.

"What paint do you use?" asked Alan, fingering the freshly-coated stern.

"Marine Counterbrine," said Casey. "It dries quickly. That's where we've fooled the constable. He saw us painting and he won't expect the boat to be ready for the water. We're going to wheel it out right in front of his nose and just hope they won't be peeved when they find out we're beyond reach for a few hours."

"They won't mind if you bring them home a nice fresh snapper for their supper," said Madeleine. "They'll encourage you to go every day. Anyway, I can tell them where you are if they want you and they can concentrate on the rest of us until you come in." She too was trying to speak cheerfully but it was evident that she had not slept well. Her face was strained and her blue eyes had dark shadows underneath.

"How many of you are going?"

"Brad and Bruce and I," said Casey. "Things might not seem so grim out there in mid-ocean. We fish round the south cliff." He pointed. "It would do Will good to come, but he told us he might be needed in the house. I've got an idea he really pulled out so that Bruce would go. It usually takes three to launch the boat when the sea's as high as this. Where *is* Bruce?"

"We saw him climbing the Lion a few minutes ago," Jabal told him. "We admired his style."

"Then he's late at it this morning. He generally goes for a swim at six and is up and down the Lion before seven. Poor kid. It's a damned shame he has to go through all this in the middle of his holidays." Casey frowned and Jabal saw his fist momentarily clench.

"Here he is now," said Bradley.

Bruce Harkin was walking towards them from the beach. His head was bent but his stride long and easy. He was in bathing trunks, a towel thrown round his shoulders. A tall, thin boy with a long face which wore a naturally serious expression, he gave no indication of his thoughts as he stopped beside them. Nor did he show any sign of breathlessness after his climb. He had the same dark hair and blue eyes as his brothers, but fair skin like that of Madeleine. In response to years of sun it had freckled rather than tanned. Jabal and Alan had met him and spoken with him before, but now looked at him as a potential murderer.

"Good-morning, Mr Freeth, Mr Jarrett," he said politely but dully. "Are you coming with us this morning?"

"They have to play golf shortly," Casey told him, "but I hope they'll come another time."

"If there is another time. We may all be in the slammer tomorrow."

"Cut it out, Bruce." Casey's tone was sharp. "Straighten that front wheel, will you?"

"I brought your pullover, Bruce," said Bradley. "You'll need it out there if the wind gets up. And here's your lifejacket."

"Thanks, Brad." Bruce spread his towel on the tussocks and picked up the pullover. "We're all set then, are we? We'll bring you back some snapper, Mr Jarrett."

"I wouldn't count on it," said Madeleine. "They're always optimistic but all they brought back last time was a left-foot cork-soled sandal that they found floating and thought someone might be glad to recover. It decorated the front of the Lodge for a week before we threw it away."

When the men had put on their lifejackets, Jabal and Alan helped to pull the three-wheeled trailer across the tussocky downs and the soft sand to a place near the south cliff. They watched as the three others lifted off the dinghy and began hauling it through the turbulent water, straining to prevent it from spinning and overturning under the force of the waves. When they were waist-deep Bruce climbed in and started the motor. The others swam one each side, steadying the boat as best they could. The spray broke over it and over them, hiding them completely from view at times, but at last they were beyond the surf. Bradley and Casey scrambled aboard; waved goodbye and started bailing out with a tin can as Bruce increased speed.

"That must've taken some effort," commented Alan, as he and Jabal strolled back along the beach. "I thought it was going to overturn and spill all their gear. I'm glad they have the sense to wear lifejackets. They must be drenched through already."

"Yes, no wonder they wear bathing trunks and woollen pullovers. I feel flattered that they invited us to go with them. They can't consider us geriatrics. It would've been an interesting experience getting into that boat. Did you notice that Madeleine showed no concern at their going out through this high surf? Apparently they're well used to it and all of them, even the boy, show considerable strength." Jabal was thinking, as he guessed Alan also was, how little of that strength would be needed to push a well honed knife from below a man's ribs up into his heart. "I wonder why Will changed his mind about going today?"

"Possibly, as Casey suggested, so that Bruce would have a distraction to take his mind off the murder."

"It will take more than that to distract him if he killed Cowan himself."

Madeleine was waiting for them in front of the cottage. "I've told the constable where they've gone," she said. "He didn't seem to care. I made some scones this morning. Would you like some?"

"Very much," said Alan. "Canon Cumbit will be particularly grateful. He has a weakness for date scones."

"Oh, has he? These are cheese, but please tell him I'll make a point of putting dates in the next lot. Come on over and get some." She managed to speak lightly but could not disguise her underlying tension. She led them across to the Harkins' kitchen. "Do you cook your own meals?"

"Strict rotation for breakfast," explained Alan. "Lunch is a scramble, each man for himself, as we have golf matches at different times. We usually buy our evening meal from the Takeaway Bar — unless, of course, a neighbour gives us a fresh snapper. We'll have to toss to see who cooks that tonight."

Madeleine smiled. "I rather think you'll be patronising the Takeaway again. There's not much snapper to be caught now. The trawlers come in too close and get it all. The boys have just gone out to get away from the atmosphere here, I think. If they were really keen on eating fish they could throw a line for some of the weed eaters round the rocks, or collect mussels."

"Do you have no chance to get away from it all yourself?"

"They never let me go with them in the boat, just in case there's an accident. They're much stronger swimmers than I am."

Alan looked at her keenly. "Are you — are you all right, my dear? Is there anything we can do to help?"

Madeleine shook her head. "Thanks, but no. No one can help. I'm all right. It's worse for Roma. Poor

Roma, finding the body like that. She's seen enough violence without this. Her husband used to bash her about."

"Is she separated? I thought she was a widow."

"She is. But her marriage was so horrible that she won't even wear her wedding ring to remind her of it. She keeps his name. Mrs Pearce. She thought of reverting to her maiden name but it would've meant altering documents and things."

"How did he die?"

"Smashed up their car while drunk one night. It was a shock at the time, I guess, but she's better off without him. She should have left the rotter, but she's so loyal. She's awfully nice, you know. How's your golf tournament going?"

"Enjoyable, but we're badly out of practice and playing shockingly."

"Will used to play a lot of golf. He was quite an addict, and brought his handicap down to five. He kept buying books on it and poring over them in the evenings. Would you like to borrow any?"

"Very much, thank you," said Jabal. "It won't really do us much good at this stage but the psychological effect of studying them is stimulating."

"I'll look them out and bring them over." She was placing scones in a bowl as she spoke. "There. And please tell Canon Cumbit he shall have his date ones. I'm going to make another batch later, mainly for those poor policemen."

"That's turning the other cheek," observed Alan.

"Not really. We all understand that they have their job to do and they're being very considerate on the whole. Of course it's horrible being finger-printed and questioned and re-questioned and having every statement queried as if you're telling lies. And not being able to go away from the premises, even to the store, without asking permission and reporting back on return. It is awful. But they could be unpleasant about it and they're not. They give the impression of being very sorry for all of us who did *not* kill Graham. Inspector Chambers is really friendly."

And that's just when he's at his most deadly, thought Jabal. But he merely said, "He's a competent officer. He'll get to the truth."

"Do you think they'll regard an offering of scones as a bribe? As if I'm saying 'Leave me alone, stop questioning me, let me go out when I please and kindly overlook the fact that I stabbed a man to death yesterday'?" Her laugh had a tinge of hysteria in it.

"I don't think they'll misjudge your motives," said Alan.

Jabal agreed. "Of course not. They'll be very grateful, especially the detectives. They often spend sixteen to eighteen hours a day on the site of a crime, because everything has to be done early. If they miss something or forget to check an object, they can't come back once they've packed up and taken their caravan away. It's too late then."

"All right then, I'll risk it. Date scones it is. Oh, here's Bradley's mother. You've met her, haven't you?"

Mrs Irma Sayer was a woman in the late forties, still handsome, slim and active. She wore slacks and a tailored blouse. Her hair was naturally curly, cut short and neatly trimmed, her features regular and discreetly made-up. In spite of her casual dress, she exuded an air of elegance and fashion. Indeed, tidiness was her daily goal in the Harkin house, a source of slight friction between her and Madeleine. She spoke briskly. "Good-morning. I've been for a walk down the beach and I swear that constable in front of the section watched me all the way. Isn't this a dreadful business? Just because some drunken hooligan wandered in and attacked poor Mr Cowan, they want to blame us for it. It's outrageous. We could sue them for damages."

Madeleine gave a small sigh of

73

impatience. "We can't kid ourselves, Irma. No one came in. The linesmen would have seen any stranger."

"Huh! Not them. They'd be too busy reading their race books or their comics and playing poker in working hours at the taxpayers' expense. I know their type. Lazy lot."

"I don't think they'd be playing poker up the telegraph poles," said Madeleine quietly. Then she changed the subject. "The boys have gone fishing," she said with false brightness. "How would you like snapper for dinner tonight?"

"What a hope. The bay's fished out and they know it. I can't see why they insist on taking that boat out. It takes an army to launch it and it's just as pleasant throwing a line from the rocks."

"And just as successful when you do it," said Madeleine. She explained to the men, "Irma has her own favourite spot the other side of the Lion. There's a little inlet there, just near the cave.

It's cut off when the tide comes in but she climbs back over the Rock if she can't get round the base. I don't know how she does it."

"It keeps me fit," said Mrs Sayer. "You should take more exercise yourself, girl, if you want to keep your figure. You'll be sorry one day that you lounge around as you do, won't she, Reverend? As a matter of fact, I might take the boat out myself one day. If they can do it, so can I. There's only small stuff round the Lion — parore mostly. The way Bradley spoke I was hoping for some big game fishing here. That's what I like. Came prepared for some really good catches."

"Irma's a keen fisherman," said Madeleine. "She's won a few competitions up North. So it's disappointing for her here."

"No matter," said Mrs Sayer. "I keep trying, and climbing back over the Rock never worries me. I like to keep active. Can't stand idleness." She addressed Alan. "Have you climbed the Rock yet, Reverend?"

"Not this time. We've all been to Piha before and climbed it at some stage, but Canon Cumbit is not so active now and wants to reserve his energy for his golf matches. We've been playing each day so far."

"The climb's nothing if you're fit. Eight minutes up, six minutes down. You should all go up again and have another look at the pa remains."

"Why should they?" asked Madeleine. "They've seen it before."

"Most people have an intelligent interest in the history of the region. Don't judge others by yourself, my girl. I'm sure Mr Jarrett and Mr Freeth don't share your apathy. That's the trouble of being brought up in an historic area such as this. You tend to forget its associations with the past. It's the tourists from overseas who can tell you about the old tribal wars and the saw-milling days and show you where the first tramway operated to

76

take the logs out. Fascinating. I read a couple of books on it before I came. The bay's teeming with legend and history." Mrs Sayer moved over to the sink and began rinsing and stacking the few dishes which were lying on the bench.

"I'll do those, Irma."

"When you get round to it, eh? Let's get them out of the way now. I can't bear dirty dishes left about. It's slovenly. I don't mind doing them. It won't take me a minute. You could be useful making us all a cup of tea, what about that? You'll have one with us, won't you Reverend? And you, vicar?"

Alan said, "No, thank you, Mrs Sayer. We must go and get ready for our golf matches."

"How's it going? Carrying off all the trophies? I've got a few cups myself, you know. I play at the Titirangi course. When I get time, that is. I'm drawn into so many other things. They *will* put me on the committees — say they can't manage without me, though I'm sure they could. My son talked me into coming here with him for a rest. A rest! I'm not the type to rest. Always on the go, I'm afraid. But there's plenty to do here."

"You didn't know what you were getting into, did you?" said Madeleine. "You'll be anxious to go home."

"Certainly not. I'll stay while I'm needed. Someone's got to keep things running smoothly while there's all this kerfuffle. What do you think about it all, Reverend?"

"I'm very sorry about the trouble you're having," said Alan. "We'd better go now. Thank you for the scones, Madeleine. We'll give the canon your kind message."

As they walked back to the cottage, he remarked, "I greatly fear, Jabal, that my tolerance is slipping. I do not like that woman Sayer."

Jabal laughed. "You're just annoyed at being called 'Reverend'. She's all right. The hearty type and proud of her fitness. Why not? If she climbs the Lion in eight minutes, she has reason to be." But as he spoke he had an uncomfortable feeling that he shared Alan's opinion.

5

"HAVE you ever felt like a piece of soap being whirled round and round before it goes down the plug hole?"

"As bad as that, is it?" Jabal looked with sympathy at their morning visitor.

"It's utterly horrible," said Madeleine. "We were happy last week. Now look at us. We're all beastly miserable and making an effort not to show it and passing silly trivial remarks about things that don't matter because we don't like to mention the things that do matter and trying to keep busy all day so we won't have time to sit and mope and each of us knowing the rest of us feel just the same as we do and the filthy rotten sun up there keeps on shining as if nothing at all had happened."

Jabal smiled at her. "And that hurts? You'd prefer *a day of darkness and of*

80

gloominess, a day of clouds and of thick darkness? I think I can understand how you feel. We're always so conscious of our own troubles that we expect the elements to reflect our mood. After all, they did it for Macbeth and they did it for Heathcliff. But they won't do it for you, Madeleine. Don't expect a stage setting for the grief. So why not try to let *your* behaviour and *your* mood echo that of Nature? The toitois are dancing in the breeze, the birds are singing, the sea is sparkling. Why put the onus on Nature to provide a correlation? Do it yourself."

"Then I'd have to scowl every time it rained and start to sob in a thunderstorm. No, thank you. I don't like that theory at all. And just what could I possibly find to be happy about today?"

It was not the moment for a sermon on the wisdom of counting one's blessings. Jabal looked with concern at her pale face and red-rimmed eyes and wished he could help. It was Alan who tried to lighten the conversation. He suggested, "Put your mind on the pleasure these scones will give Canon Cumbit when he comes home and of the improvement you will be instrumental in making to our golf by providing this book."

Madeleine gave a wan smile. "It's the only one I could find. Sorry about that. Will thinks he must've given all the others away. But this was the one he always referred to. His golf Bible, he called it. So I hope it helps. Mr Jarrett, Inspector Chambers told me that you're a sort of detective."

"I'm a vicar, Madeleine. I have a parish in Auckland."

"Yes, I know that, but he said you were very clever about summing up people and finding out who'd done what and if you could be persuaded to help you'd soon find out the truth about Graham Cowan's death."

You sidewinder. Trevor, thought Jabal. Wait till I get my hands on you.

Madeleine went on, "You see, we'd all rather know. We talked about it last night. At first we hoped no one would ever find out who killed him and that the police would give up and go away and leave us alone. Then we imagined what it would be like if they did, how we'd be looking at one another with suspicion for the rest of our lives and never being sure. It would be better to know what really happened. And there may be some — what do you call it? — extenuating circumstances. Graham could've made someone so hopping mad that they just grabbed the knife and stuck it into him in a fit of rage. We Harkins all have bad tempers. I asked Brad how he'd feel if he found out I'd done it and if I was hauled away by the police and was tried and sentenced to life imprisonment. He thought hard — he's awfully honest, Brad — and he said it'd be a shock but it wouldn't stop him loving me. He'd engage the best defence lawyer in Auckland and try to get me off with

83

manslaughter and we'd be married the day I came out of jail. Then we considered in turn how each of us would feel if one of us was guilty."

"And one of you is," said Alan. "You must face that fact, my dear."

She nodded. "Oh, I know. We all do. Even Irma now. She fought against it at first, but we discussed all possible ways someone else could've got into the shed and then we had to admit that no one did. You see, there were those linesmen your side of the Lodge, and whatever Irma thinks, linesmen don't really play cards or read race books up at the top of a telegraph pole, it would be too uncomfortable, and the boat and trailer took up nearly all the space the other side, between our house and the big corrugated iron fence on the boundary and Bruce and Casey say there was always *one* of them there and they couldn't have missed anyone squeezing past the boat — how could they? Besides, Irma was working in the kitchen most of the

84

time — she *will* clean things and tidy up and rearrange things. Do you know she won't let me leave a single dirty cup overnight? Well, she would have seen anyone passing the window, she says, even if they did get by the boat. We tried hard enough, but we couldn't put the blame on any outsider. Then Irma said wouldn't it be better for all if whoever did it gave himself up to the police because it was just a matter of time anyway? That made sense. We all agreed. But no one said they would. Whoever killed Graham must be just hoping and hoping and feeling miserable."

"How would that guilty person feel if someone else were arrested and charged?" asked Jabal.

"We discussed that too. I just couldn't bear Brad or one of my brothers to go to prison if I'd done it. At least I think I couldn't. But you can't tell, can you? You see, I *didn't* do it and I might feel differently if I had. I might be so afraid that I'd be willing to let someone else be blamed and punished. You can be so selfish when you're scared. Once when I was at school the whole class had to stay in because I wouldn't own up that I'd broken a light bulb. I was scared of what would happen to me. Then I did, because the other kids were all looking daggers at me and I was scared of them. The teacher let me off, actually. She said it was honest of me to own up, but it wasn't. If the rest of the class hadn't known I did it, I would never have said I did. I'd have let them all stay in."

"How old were you?"

"Eight."

Jabal laughed. "Then I don't think you need let that weigh on your conscience. How old are you now, Madeleine?"

"Twenty. Not quite twenty-one. Oh. Does that mean I'd get off more lightly than the others if I'd done it?" Her face was suddenly eager and her blue eyes lit up.

Jabal spoke firmly. "If you have any silly idea of confessing in order to save one of your brothers, forget it. You would not really be helping him. Remember what you discussed last night, the effects of not knowing the truth. A life sentence these days can be reduced to twelve years or less for good behaviour and as you said, it's not known what provocation prompted the attack. A verdict of manslaughter could be reached." He did not add that under New Zealand law, the lesser crime of manslaughter can bring a sentence of imprisonment for life. He changed the subject by asking, "Where are the rest of your family this morning?"

"Will's in his office doing accounts."

"Do you always call him Will? Or is it sometimes Bill?"

Madeleine looked a little surprised at the question but answered, "I always call him Will now."

"Now? Was he ever known as Bill?"

"Oh yes, when Bruce and I were kids. But he and Casey used to call me

'Mad' to tease me because they knew I hated it. Aren't big brothers cruel? So I called him Willie, hoping to annoy him, only it didn't. Somehow the Will stuck. Brad sometimes calls him Bill and so do a few others. Why do you ask?"

"It interests me. Did Graham Cowan also call him Bill?"

"I didn't hear him say 'Bill'. But he was Brad's friend so he might have. Does it matter?"

"I've been wondering, because most Williams I know have become Bill to their friends." The reason was a weak one and Madeleine still looked puzzled. Jabal went on quickly, "And I suppose you're used to being called 'Mad' now?"

"Only my brothers call me that and I have to put up with it from them. In fact if they called me Madeleine now, I'd know something was wrong, like them having the huff with me. Brad never calls me that. He knows I don't like it, but he calls me Maddy at times. I don't mind Maddy."

"Did Cowan call you Mad?"

"Oh no. He wouldn't have risked offending me." She grimaced. "He always said Madeleine, when it wasn't 'Sweet one' or 'Princess' or 'Lovely lady' or something equally silly. Isn't it awful when you don't like a person and then they die? You feel so dreadful because you're not as sorry as you think you ought to be."

She looked near to tears, so Jabal said, "You were telling me how the others are spending this bright sunny morning?"

"Brad and Case have gone off with their surf boards. Oh, and they said tell you sorry there was no fish and they'll try again. Bruce isn't back from his rock climb — he doesn't go so early now. He hasn't got the same zip, poor Brucie — and Irma's out fishing and Roma's busy in the Lodge. She's always working. She does far more than she needs to. I'm going back now to give her a hand. Aren't we lucky to have someone like Roma?

She's awfully nice. She's one of my best friends. *She* wouldn't kill anyone. She doesn't have a bad temper. Oh, Mr Jarrett, please will you help, like the Inspector said? We'll co-operate and cough up anything you want to know about us."

"But someone has *not* 'coughed up' what the police most want to know."

"I mean the rest of us would."

"Then tell me now, and tell me truthfully; have you any idea yourself who killed Graham Cowan?"

There was no hesitation in her answer. "No, I haven't. Honestly. Brad hasn't got a temper, nor Irma nor Roma. But we Harkins are pretty awful that way. Not Will quite so much. You know Will and Casey are half brothers to Bruce and me, don't you? We've all got some characteristics in common, though. Blue eyes are one and hot temper's another."

"And how does it affect you? I haven't yet seen you in a rage."

"Oh, I can blow my top now and

then. I'm growing out of it. I hope, but I used to be dynamite. I smashed a little friend's doll to pieces on the rocks once because she annoyed me. I can remember doing it and being in disgrace afterwards. I was shut up in my bedroom for the rest of the day. Only I climbed out of the window and went for a paddle and no one knew."

"Which of your brothers would be capable of killing under extreme provocation?"

Madeleine considered carefully this time before replying, "I can't really say. They'd all want to protect me, if Graham was being nasty about me. But *killing* him! It doesn't seem likely. Will would be more inclined to turn him off the premises — I can just see him glowering and ordering him to pack up and go and never come back. Boxer would lash out and give him a black eye. Bruce . . . I don't know about Bruce. He seems more worried than the other two. I've got an idea he knows something he's not telling, but that doesn't mean he did it. He really hated Graham and I guess he's just upset, as I am, because of a nasty niggling little hint of satisfaction that he's not around any more to be a nuisance. I don't think Bruce is the one who stabbed him."

"You said 'Boxer' who's that?"

"I meant Casey."

"Why did you call him 'Boxer'? Has he done some boxing?"

"Yes, quite a bit, but he came to be called that because he . . . I suppose you'd better know. It was because he used to fight such a lot at school and that's where he got the nickname. Will says his first reaction if another boy riled him was to push his face in and that he was always getting into trouble for starting a scrap. That's what he'd have done to Graham, too, if Graham made him mad. Push his face in, that's all. Not use a knife. He's so kind really, dear old Boxer. He won't even poison rats and he brings in gulls when they're hurt and . . . " She stopped. Then with an effort at self-control she said primly, "We'd be very grateful if you could help find out what really happened, Mr Jarrett. Please think about it. I'll go back now and help Roma."

Jabal merely said, "Thank you for the scones and the book."

When she had left, Alan turned to him. "That poor child! So Casey Harkin is nicknamed Boxer and William is occasionally called Bill. Your suspects are increased to three. Surely you'll be willing to lend a hand now?"

"It certainly complicates the case for Trevor. We must let him know."

"According to your theories, the one most likely to have stabbed Cowan will be the one who did it. Well? Which was it? Which one, at this stage, do you consider to be the most likely?"

"Bruce had the motive, Casey the temperament, Will the best opportunity. It was one of the three."

"*Which* one, Jabal?"

"All right, you win. I'll talk to them and I'll have a guess. That's all I can do and that's all I undertake to do. I'm not the detective that Trevor makes me out to be. I have no special talents in that direction. But every person reveals himself as he talks. A man can remain a mystery, an enigma, until he opens his mouth. *Even a fool, when he holdeth his peace, is counted wise, and he that shutteth his lips is esteemed a man of understanding.* It's just as well that criminals seldom remember that. They chatter and they give themselves away. In *time*. It takes time, but even the most superficial trivial conversation is guided by the personalities of the participants."

"It was trivial enough yesterday when we went over to the boat and made small talk about paint and fishing and food. Did you get anything from that?"

"Of course. Even what people *don't* say is significant during a conversation, and the most mundane subjects can still give an indication not only of character, but of a person's past and present activities. One killer I knew gave himself away by referring to a woman in the past tense, when her body had not yet been found. It was a natural slip to make. You formed certain conclusions yourself, Alan, during that idle chatter yesterday. You must have. What were they?"

"I didn't even think of drawing conclusions."

"Then do it now. Put your mind back onto what was said and what you can deduce from it."

"Is that the way you do it? Well . . . let me think. Madeleine offered to lend us her brother's golf books without asking his permission. That shows how well they all get on together."

"Or a sneaky underhand tendency?"

"Of course not. They were all concerned for one another."

"Or pretending to be."

"Mrs Sayer has courage. She's not afraid of anything. She said if the men could take the boat out, so could she."

"She said that only a minute after

remarking that she couldn't understand why they took the boat out, that it was just as pleasant fishing from the rocks. If she feels the need to emphasise her courage, there may be an underlying sense of inadequacey. But go on, what else?"

"Casey showed some prejudice. He talked about having to fool the constable and he said reporters print lies if they don't like you. Madeleine displays a concern for others. She asked how we managed for meals, and how our tournament was getting on and she was sorry for the policemen. All right, all right, — she *said* she was. It may have been the result of a desire to conceal her worry and to stop us from asking questions."

"Fine. You're getting the idea."

"Yes, I think I am. Casey and Bradley showed — or pretended — a special sympathy for Bruce. It appears that they look after him and are worried about the effect of this tragedy on him. Mrs Sayer said she'd stay while she was needed. I still find it difficult to like that woman, but she shows a sense of duty. That's also evident in her being on so many committees. I wonder why Madeleine referred to her as a keen 'fisher*man*'? Does that show a masculine quality in Mrs Sayer? I noticed yesterday that Madeleine avoided a direct argument with her, but she wasn't too meek. Remember, she said why should we go up the Lion to look at the pa remains? I have a feeling that she'd be a match for Mrs Sayer any day, but the woman's a guest in her house and she accordingly treats her with tolerance and courtesy. How am I doing?"

"Excellent. Carry on. What else did you notice about Madeleine?"

"She told us about her friend Roma's unhappy marriage, and we're still comparative strangers to them both. A fondness for gossip? Or just a frank open nature, with no secrets in her own life, so assuming everyone else's is an open book? I also remarked a slight tendency to smooth over any disagreement before it could develop. She may be accustomed to acting as a peacemaker. She's grown up with brothers reputed to be bad-tempered."

"As she admits to being herself. They all assume that Cowan was killed in a fit of rage, but perhaps the police have let that theory be known."

"They want it to be that, because they want to be able to excuse the one that did it. They seem attached to one another. Casey assumed that Will had decided not to go fishing, so that Bruce would go instead. Yet their apparent affection could all be a pretence, covering up a deep underlying hatred. How's that?"

"You see, you're just as capable as I am, and probably more so, of making deductions from idle chatter. We've formed impressions of each one's personality. We can't tell yet how correct those impressions are. The personality presented to us may be one deliberately projected onto our mental receiving screen. If it was, that in itself tells us something. I think we should try to find out more about Cowan himself, because the character of the victim is often a guide to his killer. It may provide us with the motive for his murder, and the motive of a crime leads to its perpetrator."

"How do we find out about him?"

"The same way. Encourage talk. Sound the others, all of them, not just the three suspects, on their opinion of the dead man. Bradley Sayer knew him best. I suggest you start with him."

"We start with him," corrected the archdeacon. "I wasn't proposing to relieve you of what you now know is your duty. But I'm willing to follow your methods and try to emulate your skill at deduction. We must get George onto it, too. He's a shrewd judge of character. We'll sum up each of the brothers and decide which one was the murderer of Cowan. Oh dear, how confusing if we each choose a different one!"

6

"WE have some results from the DSIR. I thought you might be interested." Detective-Inspector Trevor Chambers looked doubtfully at Jabal. But his reception was not what he expected.

"Come in, Inspector," called Archdeacon Freeth.

"Sit down," invited Canon Cumbit.

"Anything useful?" enquired Jabal.

"A few facts which may help. The blow was an upwards thrust, as we decided, but delivered, it's thought, by a left hand. That doesn't necessarily indicate a left-handed killer, as a stab like that would need strength more than dexterity. It does suggest a person accustomed to using both hands more than the normal man."

"Like a boxer?" suggested Alan.

"Any manual worker, really. Only

one of the household signed a statement with the left hand, and that was Mrs Sayer, so that doesn't help. It's been suggested that the left hand might have been used if the assailant was holding something in his right."

"A fish?" suggested George. "You'd think he'd put it down first."

"It's more probable that both hands were used, with the left one dominant. It would be natural and more effective to hold the knife with both hands." The Inspector took up a table knife and demonstrated. "Like this, see?"

Alan took out his ballpoint pen and experimented. "You're right. More force that way."

"Lend me your pen," said George. "Hm . . . yes. You'd have to use both hands for a really good shove. It's something like wielding a cricket bat."

Trevor Chambers looked with mild surprise at them both. "I'm glad you two are taking an interest. Has Jabal been getting at you? As you say, the action in handling a large knife for

101

such a purpose as this would be similar to that required for wielding a cricket bat or any sporting implement. Young Bruce Harkin plays hockey for his school in winter and cricket in summer. Casey works in the garage that he owns and a mechanic needs both hands for his job. Of course, it's not much to go on. The knife was fingerprinted, but the handle had been wiped clean, as we expected. There were two prints on the blade near the hilt — one of Mrs Sayers right thumb, partially superimposed by one of Roma Pearce's forefinger. As Mrs Sayer used the knife to clean fish with it on the morning of the stabbing, and Mrs Pearce touched it briefly when she discovered the body, those prints are also of no significance. Have you discovered anything useful yourselves?"

Jabal told him, "We've learned, purely by chance, that Casey Harkin is nicknamed Boxer and that William was called Bill as a boy and is still known as that to some of his friends. Madeleine admits that Cowan could've heard him referred to as Bill before he came here and could also hear Bradley use that name for him now and then."

"Ah! So it's Bruce, Boxer and possibly Bill. Not as simple as you claimed it was, Jabe."

"Three possibles instead of two," conceded Jabal.

Alan said, "But would Cowan be about to say 'Boxer'? He didn't know Casey well. It was the first time he'd come here, according to Will. Would he use a family nickname?"

"He'd give the name easiest to say," said Jabal. "He knew he had very little time. Do you remember, Madeleine said he never called her 'Mad' to her face? But a three-syllabled name would not be used when one syllable would do. Each word was an effort for him. He'd heard the others call her 'Mad' and presumably he'd heard them refer to Casey as 'Boxer'. Either name might have occurred to him in those last few stressful moments."

George said, "Yet 'Will' is as simple to say as 'Bill', and 'Bill' was seldom used for William Harkin. So it's unlikely that he was about to say 'Bill'."

"That's true," said the Inspector, "and we're inclined to eliminate William for other reasons. He appears to be a more restrained type than his brothers, his sedentary work would develop only the right hand — he studied accountancy and worked for a firm in the city before he took over this place — and the fact that he was going in and out of the shed that afternoon would surely suggest to him that any attack on Cowan in the shed would be attributed to him. That knowledge would deter him. He's not a fool."

"But it could've been a sudden, impromptu attack."

"Oh, it was. We're fairly sure of that. But even in a fit of anger, Will would've known he'd be first suspect."

"But he isn't," Jabal pointed out. "Besides, one doesn't stop to reason out such matters in a fit of anger."

"No, I suppose not. We can't rule him out altogether. But he seems less likely to have done it than the other two."

"Madeleine's worried about Bruce," Jabal said. "She thinks he's holding something back, that he knows more than he's told. It could be simple guilt affecting him. But he's not as strong as Casey. More agile, perhaps, but not as muscular."

"Strength isn't an essential factor," Trevor told him. "I said it was more important than dexterity, but only moderate strength would be required. The knife was kept very sharp, the Harkins say. Cowan was wearing a cotton T-shirt and no vest, and there's very little effort needed to push a sharp knife into the human body if bones are avoided and clothes penetrable. It's pulling one out that's difficult. That's why the weapon is so often left in a stabbed victim. The killer tries to pull it out. He doesn't want to lose his favourite knife. He might wish to use it next day on someone else. But he finds to his surprise that it won't come and he can't afford the time to stop and wrestle with it. Bayonet victims in the war had sometimes to be shot before the blade could be withdrawn. I don't think in this case that any effort was made. There was no sign of it."

"If you don't need strength to put a knife in," asked George, "why is Casey's manual work important?"

"It's a factor only in indicating familiarity in using both hands, not as development of muscular strength."

Jabal asked, "Have you any information on Cowan himself?"

"Yes. He has a police record. He was convicted and fined in '79 for growing cannabis in the Waitakeres. He was unmarried, lived alone in his Titirangi home — an expensively built modern house, no mortgage on it — travelled extensively, had various business investments. You can read through the list, Jabal, if you think it'll help. I've told the boys you're to have access to any information we get, and providing I'm with you it'll be in order for you to read the files. By the way, we've finished in the shed. The family can start using it again. I'll go and tell Harkin now." He got to his feet. "I drove out at dawn this morning and it'll be dark when I return to Auckland."

When Chambers had left, Alan remarked, "That last comment was an appeal to your sympathy, Jabal, a further plea for help. You'll have to get busy. Personally, I've already made up my mind. It was obviously the young fellow who did it. Bruce."

"No," said George. "It was the other one — Boxer or Casey or whatever they call him. It must have been him. Don't you agree, Jabal?"

"I have no definite opinion as yet. There's much research to be done." Jabal was looking out the window as he spoke. "I see Roma Pearce out there picking flowers. It's very fortunate for her that Cowan spoke before he died.

She found the body, her fingerprint was on the blade of the knife, she would have several excuses for going into the shed, and her late husband used to knock her about. Violence sometimes begets violence. So Cowan has saved her much harassment by the police. I think I'll go over and have a chat with her to see what her own opinion is on the matter."

"So that's how you go about it?" asked Alan. "You just get each person to give his or her views on the subject, like taking an opinion poll. Then you point the finger at the unfortunate suspect whom nobody loves."

"Not at all. But another person's opinion of a man reflects the impact of that man's personality and his personality cannot fail to provide some indication of his guilt or innocence. Besides, in expressing one's views on a fellow being, one reveals much of oneself. As I said, it's not only the character of the three suspects which we must examine. We need to know how each of those involved has reacted, what they think, what they feel. That is important in order to get a general picture, a picture which, as it's enlarged, will eventually show us which of the three men is the killer."

"I think we'd better go with him, Alan," said the canon. "We can study his methods. Then you can do some moonlighting as a private eye when you get sick of counting the hymn books. May we come, Jabal?"

"Certainly. Roma's not a suspect and I doubt if she has any guilty secrets to confess, even if she chose me to confide in. The conversation will be superficial, but it may nevertheless be helpful, and I'd be glad of your assistance."

Roma Pearce was cutting blue and white agapanthus on the slope by the Lodge. She straightened up and greeted them with a polite "Good-morning." She looked tired but composed. "How's the golf?"

"Enjoyable, thank you," replied Jabal, "though not yet very successful. But

Madeleine has lent us Will's book on the subject and we intend to analyse and correct our faults from it this evening, with a view to annihilating the opposition tomorrow."

"I hope you do. I'm told Will was a five handicap in his day but he's hardly played at all since I've been here. He's always too busy. He works too hard. I wish he'd go out for a round or two. It would do him good, especially now, when he's so worried. Of course we all are. I wish the police would hurry up and get it over with."

"Even though that would mean arrest of one of the household?"

"Yes. We talked about that the other evening. Irma Sayer hinted that it was the duty of whoever did it to own up and I think she's right. I think whoever did it *will* own up. It must take some courage but they'll do it in time. They wouldn't let the others go on suffering."

"Who wouldn't? Do you know, Mrs Pearce?"

"Goodness, no. I'm not even guessing who. They're all so decent. They've been awfully good to me, especially Will. I was in a pretty low state when I came here. I must have been the least suitable applicant for the job, but I told him my circumstances and why I wanted it and I'm sure he chose me because he thought I was the one who needed it most. I made up my mind he'd never regret it. I certainly don't. It's a pleasure to work hard for them, they're all so nice. They treat me like one of the family, and Madeleine's a dear. She's become one of my best friends."

"Did anyone object to the suggestion of the culprit owning up?"

"N-no. Not really. Bruce said it wouldn't happen."

"Why? Did he give a reason?"

"No. He's very depressed and I guess he was just being pessimistic. I think it's hit him harder than anyone."

"Did he do it himself?"

To Jabal's surprise, Roma showed

111

no indignation or even disquiet at the question. She said calmly, "It's possible. He didn't like Graham. He had a real row with him last week. I heard them yelling at each other, though I don't know what it was about. And something's bugging him at present, besides the natural effect of having someone murdered on the property, I mean. I feel Bruce has something else on his mind. Here he is now. Look, coming up from the beach. He's late this morning. It's after ten. Do you see what I mean? He doesn't even run as he used to. He's slumping along with his head down, like an old man. It's more than just the reaction you'd expect from a kid. Do you think he'd tell one of you what the matter is?"

"He would be more likely to confide his trouble to one of his family, wouldn't he?" asked Alan.

"Not necessarily," said Jabal. "It's often easier to talk to a stranger, one with whom there are no emotional ties.

He's too close to his family, too much aware of the effect on them of what he may say. He doesn't have to consider our feelings, as he would theirs. When we leave here he will probably never see us again. Their lives will always be wrapped up with his own. Yes, I'll go and have a word with the boy."

He walked up the beach to meet Bruce. Alan and George, with years of experience themselves in hearing confidences and offering counsel, knew better than to follow. They continued talking to Roma, hoping to learn facts which they could later report to Jabal.

Bruce did not seem to be aware of anyone else near him until Jabal spoke. "Hullo, Bruce."

The boy looked up then and Jabal was startled at his appearance. In only a few days the flush of youth had gone. His face, by nature lean, was now almost gaunt, and the strain of worry showed in its tight drawn muscles. "Good-morning, Mr Jarrett," he replied mechanically, listlessly.

Jabal decided not to hedge round the point. Most of the teenagers he had dealings with preferred straight talking, as he did himself. He said, "Bruce, what do you know about this terrible affair?"

Bruce didn't tell him to mind his own business. He said dully, "Oh yes, Mad said you were going to help get to the bottom of it."

"I can't promise that. I'll try, and you can best help by telling me everything you know." Before the boy could protest that he knew nothing, Jabal went on, "I want to ask you something, but before I do, I would remind you of my calling. We do not betray confidences and anything you say to me will remain with me unless I have your permission to repeat it."

"You can ask me anything. Mad says you're a private detective."

"I'm not a detective. I am, above all, a priest, used to hearing other people's troubles and trying to help. It's true that Inspector Chambers is a personal

114

friend and that I've worked with him at times in some of his cases. If I can help him untangle this one, I'd like to do so. That's partly the reason I'm talking to you now. But, I repeat, I do not betray confidences, even to the police. Do you understand?"

Bruce regarded him earnestly. "Yes, I think I do. You mean that what I say may give you some idea of who killed Graham and then you can go about proving it but you won't tell anyone else what I say to you?"

"Not without your consent."

"I see. That sounds fair. But there's nothing I'd say that you couldn't repeat."

"I feel something more than the actual murder is worrying you." Bruce made no reply and Jabal continued, "This is a dreadful situation you're all plunged into. The police will eventually discover who killed Mr Cowan. That's inevitable. They won't give up until they do. It would be better for all concerned if the culprit were to own up and save this extended suffering, not only better for others, but for himself as well. Every day brings further worry and tension and unhappiness. Don't you agree?"

The boy nodded. "Yes, I do."

"Then I'll ask you now — did you stab Graham Cowan?"

Bruce answered readily and with no sign of resentment at the suggestion. "No, I didn't. I hated his guts but I didn't kill him. I *would* own up if I had. I'd do anything to get Will and Boxer out of it all. *Anything.*"

"They're good brothers to you?"

"The very best."

"Why did you hate Cowan?"

"He was slimy, smarmy, and he kept trying to do a line with Mad."

"You're fond of your sister?"

"Mad? She's a good sort. We get on well. I didn't like him pestering her all the time. And he was beastly about Bradley too. He said horrible things about him and they weren't true. Brad's not like that. He's an awfully decent chap."

"What things did Cowan say?"

"He told me Brad was dishonest and not good enough for Mad and that if she knew more about him she'd soon give him the brush off. He said that to *me*. So I guess he told everyone else the same sort of thing. He hinted to me that Brad had done something awful once and that *he* was being kind in not telling anyone about it. I asked him what it was and he wouldn't say. He said it wouldn't be fair to Brad. It would be unkind to tell me or anyone. The beastly hypocrite. He didn't mind hinting, which was just as bad."

"Did you ask Bradley about it?"

"No. I thought it would be insulting even to mention the rubbish Graham talked. Brad wouldn't do anything shady. He's super. He really is."

"I hear you had a stand-up row with Cowan one day?"

"More than one day." Bruce gave a weak smile. "I told him to lay off Mad and he told me to mind my own

117

business. We were always rowing but not for long at a time because he'd treat me like a small boy being cheeky to an adult. Sort of condescending but tolerant, not wanting to quarrel with a schoolboy. That made me madder than ever. He was a real beast. But I didn't kill him."

"Do you know who did?"

Bruce was silent. Jabal felt acute sympathy for him as he saw the anguish on his face. After a few seconds, Bruce answered, "I know which one of them would not own up. That's all."

"Can you tell me?"

"I'd better not. It's just my own opinion."

"Do you feel like talking to the police?"

"I would if I had any facts to give them, if I'd heard or seen anything I could report. I'd go straight to them — really I would — to save Mad going through all this. She doesn't deserve it. But I've nothing to tell them. It's just that I *know* everyone and I'm pretty sure there's only one who'd keep quiet. Owning up would be the best thing to do, like you said. It's just a matter of time so it would hurry things up."

"It would be best for all concerned," agreed Jabal.

"I'm awfully glad you're going to help, Mr Jarrett. I haven't said anything you can't repeat. But then, I haven't been able to tell you anything useful, have I? Not yet, anyway. But I have a sort of an idea. Look, if I find out anything, I'll let you know, shall I?"

"Thank you," said Jabal. "I'd be glad if you would. Now tell me, what was your time up the Lion this morning?"

"I don't know. I'd taken my watch off for surfing. I haven't timed myself for ages and I don't think I could be bothered just now. It's not fun any more, going up the Rock. I just keep doing it each day because it's a habit."

"And a very good one. I was most impressed with your style. Would you like me to time you one morning?"

"Oh. Righto. Thanks," said Bruce, with no enthusiasm.

"When would it suit you?"

"Any day. I don't care."

"We have to make an early start tomorrow but we're free the following day until half-past ten. Would that do? Say eight o'clock? Good. Canon Cumbit has a stopwatch function on his watch, so we'll get him to bring that along. I'm going to go and have a closer look at the Lion now. I haven't climbed it for over three years. I'm interested to look at the track you take. Isn't it quicker to go up the centre front, like the rest of the world?"

"Not really," explained Bruce, with a little more animation. "The side's quicker once you've mastered it and know exactly where to put your feet and where to cling on with your hands. It's shorter in distance, but it's dangerous for tourists. That's partly why I usually go up so early. Will doesn't like visitors to see me climbing in case one tries to go the same way and kills himself.

One did watch last summer and later decided to have a go at it himself. Luckily Casey saw him and ran over to give him a talking to, about the risks of accident and so on. Case ordered him down as if it was his own property and he was a trespasser. When Boxer gets mad at someone they don't argue back. They just do as he says."

"Does Casey not mind your doing it?"

"No, not now. There's really no risk for me and he knows that. I'm so used to it. I have my own set track, footholds and handholds, and I'm not stupid."

"You're certainly not," said Jabal. "I shall look forward to seeing your skill the day after tomorrow."

As he walked towards the Lion, he turned once to look back. Bruce was lumbering slowly up the beach, head bent and feet dragging.

7

JABAL stood on the summit of the
Lion Rock and looked about him.
It was several years since he had last
visited Piha. A few more homes had
been built since then, roofs renewed,
sections cultivated, walls and fences
painted, roads improved. But little else
had changed. The same rugged cliffs
stood out against the blue sky, the
waves crashed with equal ferocity onto
the beach, the gunmetal sand sparkled
as ever in the sunlight. The Piha stream
wound through flax bushes and toitois
towards the Rock. Some said it was
responsible for the Rock's formation,
bringing down sediment and rubble
over the years and dumping them
at its mouth in this untidy heap
which roughly resembled the figure
of a crouching lion.

Behind the houses and holiday baches

along the shore were hills on which huge kauri trees had once stood tall. Now the kauri was so rare and so precious that it was illegal to fell one, even on one's own property, and the hills were covered with second-growth bush. The tangle of manuka, five-finger, tree-ferns, karaka, formed a screen through which the helicopter spotters found it hard to detect plantations of cannabis.

Jabal turned away, unwilling to be reminded of the drug scene. On the sea side of the Lion rose its 'fingers', short spires left after erosion of softer surrounding stone. To the north, above high tide line, was the small mound of the 'Little Lion', to the south more named rocks — the Camel, the Nun, the Wedding Cake — and over at the southern cliffs the Blowhole, where Hauauru, the god of the west wind, puffs into wisps the belchings of the fierce underground taniwha.

After walking about the remains of the Maori pa pits and terraces, looking down at each side of the Rock, admiring the view from each angle and briefly discussing the Test cricket scores with a couple of English tourists, Jabal climbed down again and found Bradley Sayer sitting on a boulder by the War Memorial set in the buttocks of the Lion. He was in bathing shorts, with a surf board on the sand beside him.

"I was waiting for you," said Bradley. "I saw you climb up. You're almost as quick as young Bruce."

"I've no temptation to take the same route," said Jabal. "He's an athletic boy, isn't he?"

"He's a nice kid."

Jabal sat down on a ledge of rock. If Bradley had waited to see him, he must want to talk. After a few moments Bradley remarked, "It's a rotten shame that he and Madeleine had to get mixed up in all this."

"It's hard on all of you."

"Maddy says you're going to help get to the bottom of it."

"I can try but I can't promise success.

I understand that Cowan was a friend of yours?"

"He was once," said Bradley, "but he was no friend lately. Look, I don't know what to do. If you're going to probe into things, there's something you'd better know. It's only a matter of time before the police find out, if they haven't already. I wondered whether to tell them before they do, only it's not really connected and if I mention it they might think it is. Do you mind if I tell you about it and see what you think?"

There was no need for Jabal to answer. Bradley had evidently made up his mind, for he went on, "It's like this. I met Graham years ago. We both lived in Titirangi and were members of the golf club there. Our standard of play was about the same so we enjoyed having a round together. But Graham was well off financially and I was scratching to get enough even for the annual sub. One day he made a suggestion to me." Bradley brushed some sand off his surf board. Then he nodded his head and said, as if assuring himself, "Yes, I do want to tell you about it. I was finishing my pharmacy course and trying to make do on a bursary. My parents had helped but they were both overseas that year and they didn't realise how much I'd had to fork out for books and fees. I was baching at home by myself and if I'd written to ask them for money they'd have got in a flap and they might have cut their holiday short. Graham offered me a loan, but I didn't want to borrow. Then he had this idea. You know what the sections at Titirangi are like? All that bush? We have two acres of it round our house. So it seemed a jolly good idea at the time."

Bradley fell silent. After a few seconds Jabal said, "What is it that you are so hesitant to tell me? Were you involved in some criminal activity?"

"Yes. Graham persuaded me to let him clear a patch of the bush and grow cannabis on it. He did the work, provided the plants and we split the profits. He harvested it that season, when the plants were still quite small, but even so, we made quite a bit out of it. Don't say anything. I know now how stupid it was. I didn't see the implications at the time. I didn't know what I was doing. It was just a way to make money."

"But you know now?" Jabal's face hardened. He had too often seen the effect of drugs, and the trade in them was a subject which never failed to disturb him.

"Yes, I know now. A bit later on I was friendly with a girl at Varsity who started on marijuana. She insisted it was no more harmful than a glass of beer."

"Then she moved on to the hard stuff?"

"How did you know? She's been in a clinic for the last two years. Some of the guys, too . . . one's dead. He was a special mate of mine. He got a

Senior Scholarship and was in line for an overseas study grant."

"Was your plantation discovered?"

"No. Graham took the crop and paid me my whack. Fifty percent, which I thought was generous of him, since he'd done all the work. I suspect now that I was taking the risks. If the cops had got onto it, he'd have skipped and left me to face the charges. As it happened, he was the one to be caught in the end. He'd put down other areas, some much larger, up in the Waitakeres, and the next year he was found out and taken to court. He got off with a fine because they thought it was a first offence. In the meantime my parents had returned from their holiday abroad and they found the patch of bush cleared. That was bad luck for me. They hardly ever went into the bush and I'd thought it would've grown back before they ever saw that portion. It was only a little piece. Well, they started asking awkward questions. They knew Graham was a friend of mine and his name was in the papers, so they put two and two together. I had to tell them. They were mad at me, of course, and they were also scared that the police would come round, because all known associates of Cowan were being investigated. But my mother always sticks by me, whatever I do, and Dad rose to the occasion too. He cleared the patch completely and enlarged it and by the time the police did come, it was planted in neat rows of grape vines. I don't think he deceived them but they couldn't prove anything and they left me alone. That was six years ago and I was forgetting all about it until just before Christmas when Graham turned up here."

"Why had he come?"

"He said for a surfing holiday, and that was probably the truth. He seemed genuinely surprised and pleased to see me. He'd moved away from Titirangi after the cannabis charge, so he couldn't have known I'd be here. He told the Harkins we were old friends and they kept inviting him to the house. It was fine at first. We got on well. He was always good company — fun to be with. But then he fell for Madeleine. He made no secret of the fact, either. And he started to pester her. When I objected he threatened to tell her about my cannabis patch."

"Blackmailing you?"

"Oh no. He had pots of money. Apart from all the profits from his business concerns, he made a pile out of the cannabis plantations that the police didn't know about. You can get up to a thousand dollars for one fully grown cannabis plant. He was actually quite generous with his money and not after any more from me. He just wanted to put Madeleine off me, and she loathes drugs, so it *would* have put her off. There's a lot of cannabis grown here now, up in the bush, and over the hill at Karekare and all the decent residents resent it because it's giving the place a bad name. I asked Graham not to tell Madeleine, but I wasn't going to crawl to him. And then . . . "

"And then he was silenced."

"Exactly. So why don't the police arrest me? They must know by now. They dig up all your past and even though I was never charged I bet the Wanganui computer has a record of my association with Graham and the visit the police made to our property. So why don't they haul me off to the cells?"

Because you're not Madeleine's brother, thought Jabal. In his last few moments, Cowan actually did you a favour. He said, "Should they?"

"By all logic, yes. I had all to gain from his death. But I didn't kill him. I know I'd say I didn't even if I did. But I didn't."

"Who did?"

"I wish I knew. Not Maddy, of course, and she must know I didn't. But everything will come out before they find out who the killer was. Madeleine will learn what I did and she hates drugs, like I told you, so she'll never forgive me."

"Why not tell her before she finds out from another source?"

"I keep hoping it won't be necessary. Oh, I'll tell her *one* day. When we've been married ten years or so and she knows I wouldn't do anything like that any more, *then* I'll tell her. It's just time I want. Time for her to get to know me and trust me."

"Even after ten years she may feel hurt that you didn't confide in her, that you kept a portion of your past hidden."

"If I told her now I'd lose her and I couldn't bear that. There's young Bruce, too. He thinks a lot of me. Sort of looks up to me, and I enjoy it. I guess I'm flattered. I don't want to lose his trust."

"Bruce may never know. He need not know. But do you really want to keep it from the woman with whom you hope to spend the rest of your life? Madeleine told me that you had a discussion one evening as to how you'd each react if one of you confessed to Cowan's murder. Did she say what her feelings would be if it were you?"

Bradley looked thoughtful. "Yes, she did. She said she'd be surprised and a bit shocked and disappointed in me but she wouldn't want to break off our engagement and when we were married she wouldn't be scared that I'd ever stick a knife in her too."

"And which do you consider the greater crime — taking the life of a fellow guest in someone else's house, or trying to make money, in ignorance, out of a suggestion made to you by a more sophisticated friend? What appears to be utter selfishness and greed in young people is often simply lack of thought and of understanding. When you're young the world is full of new and exciting possibilities, and you are the centre of it all. I loved my parents, yet I used to canoe down the Waikato without a lifejacket. It didn't occur to me that I was doing *them* any harm.

133

At that age, I considered that my life was my own affair. All the young are self-centred. Only as you grow older do you realise that in a community your life is never your own. A certain amount of risk and adventure is both desirable and necessary in youth, but stupid endangering of one's life is another thing. All my parents had asked me to do was to take a sensible, reasonable precaution — a lifejacket, which I didn't like wearing because it was uncomfortable and clumsy."

"How old were you?"

"Fifteen."

"Well, I was twenty-two. I should've had more sense by then."

"It's what you are now that matters to Madeleine. She's only twenty herself, yet I've noticed a maturity in her outlook. I think she would understand."

"Are you saying I should tell her?"

"I'm not presuming to dictate to you what you should do. You'll think out for yourself what is the best course to take. I must go and get ready for golf now. I have a match at midday."

"Good luck with it. I'll think about what you said."

Jabal left him sitting on the boulder, staring at his surf board.

8

WHEN the three golfers returned late that afternoon, they saw Bradley Sayer and his mother pulling the boat on its trailer past the front of the Lodge towards its parking site by the side of the Harkins' house.

"We'd better give them a hand," suggested Alan.

"They don't need a hand," said Jabal. "One person alone can pull that three-wheeler now that it's on the grass. It's only over the sand and the tussocks that they can do with help. I want a shower." He did not add that he had already talked to Bradley that morning.

"We can help them lift the boat off," persisted Alan.

George supported him. "Indeed we can. We should."

"They would probably prefer to leave

136

it on the trailer, ready for the next time they use it."

"It would be neighbourly to offer," said Alan.

"My shirt is sticking to me."

"We're just as hot as you are," said George. "Your personal comfort should not take precedence over your obligations. You have a job to do."

"So that's it. I thought as much. You're being devious again."

"If you come and talk with them now," said Alan more cunningly, "we might let you have first turn in the bathroom when we go inside. Right, George?"

"Agreed," said George.

"No tossing?" asked Jabal.

"No tossing, no arguments, and what's more," offered Alan, "*I* shall go and get our meal from the Takeaway."

"Done," said Jabal. They walked over to the boat, by now in its usual place. Irma Sayer looked unusually tousled and untidy. Her hair was hanging in wet, bedraggled strands, her blouse and shorts were drenched and a couple of scratches showed up red and ugly on her tanned legs.

"Mother's been out in the boat," explained Bradley. He was frowning angrily. "She launched it herself."

"In this surf?" exclaimed Alan. "That must have taken some skill."

"The sea's not as rough as usual this afternoon," said Mrs Sayer, "and there's a spot down past the Camel where the waves aren't too high. I just had to wait for the right moment. I didn't bring it in too gracefully, though. I turned the engine off too soon and the silly thing spun about and nearly capsized and one of the day-trippers in the water had to help me beach it. Jolly decent of him. I might've lost my fishing gear. I'm afraid I got a bit damp." She laughed and pulled at her soaking blouse.

"It was a silly risky thing to do," growled her son. "I was worried stiff when I knew where you were."

"There was no risk. I'm not an idiot.

I wore a lifejacket and once beyond the waves the sea was fairly calm. Just a gentle swell. I knew I could launch it. I've proved my point and I shan't want to do it again. It was worth a try — you know I prefer the big stuff to those little tiddlers I catch from the rocks. I came prepared for big game fishing," she told the others. "I brought my own gear, expecting some good sport, but I haven't been invited to go out in the boat."

"Of course not," said Bradley. "They get wet through launching that boat. They have to swim to get through the surf and then heave themselves in. It's no place for a woman."

"But I did it, didn't I?" Irma's face wore a smile of satisfaction.

"I don't know how you managed, and it was dangerous. Besides, you shouldn't have taken the Harkins' boat without their permission. You might have wrecked it."

"But I didn't, did I?"

"You didn't catch any fish either, so

it was a waste of effort."

"It's not catching fish that matters," said Irma. "It's the fun of trying to. Anyway, I did have a catch. The snapper weren't biting, or they weren't there to bite, but I got an enormous stingray on my line. I got such a surprise to see what it was. No good for eating, of course, but I thought I might as well have a bit of sport with him. He was a powerful brute, a huge thing. Wanted to pull me out of the dinghy and once he nearly did. That got my mettle up. I played the fellow for over an hour and then landed him, still alive and kicking."

"What did you do with it?" asked Alan.

"Put an end to him and threw him back. It was jolly hard work, I can tell you. Look at me. Tore my blouse and cut my wrist and got as wet as a shag, playing that chap. I'm quite exhausted. So it's sympathy I deserve, not criticism; don't you agree, Mr Jarrett?"

"My sympathies," said Jabal coldly, "are entirely with the stingray."

Alan spoke up quickly. "Did the police not mind your going out in the boat?"

"I didn't ask them. What's it got to do with them? The fellow in the front of the section saw what I was doing and he didn't object. Why should he? I couldn't go far in a small dinghy. When are those police going to get off the property? Why don't they arrest someone and have done with it, or else buzz off and leave us alone?"

"They're doing their best," said Bradley.

Jabal spoke. "Whom would you like them to arrest, Mrs Sayer?" She looked at him with a strange expression and on an impulse he asked, "Do you know who killed Cowan?"

She stared at him. It was not a friendly stare, but that was hardly to be expected after his previous remark. Then she said, with a half-smile, "Yes, I know."

"What?" exclaimed Bradley. "You know? How do you know? Who was it?"

She was still looking at Jabal as she replied, "*That* is something I am not prepared to say. It's the police's job to find out, not mine. They're the ones paid for it."

"Are you guessing?" asked Jabal. "Or have you some evidence?"

She smiled again, a slow smile, gently widening and curling her well shaped mouth. "Let us say that I know for a fact. I do not intend to discuss it. I'm going inside now to change. I look a disgrace to the bay. When I've bathed and changed I'll be in the kitchen, if you want me, Bradley. I'll give Madeleine a hand with the dinner. I want to show her how to braise the carrots instead of boiling them the way she does. And she cuts the runner beans too chunky. I hope you're enjoying your golf matches," she added, looking at Alan and then George. She ignored Jabal, obviously having no particular wish that he experience any form of enjoyment. Then she walked round the corner of the house.

"Does your mother really know who killed Cowan?" asked Jabal.

"I was just as surprised as you were when she said that," Bradley told him. "She hasn't said so before. But she was in the kitchen that afternoon, wasn't she? The window looks out on the shed and she could've seen more than she let on. Or perhaps she's discovered something since. Mother's odd in some ways. She doesn't lie — she's always taken a pride in that — and she's usually right when she makes a statement." He smiled. "That's what gets Madeleine's goat. I think. Being constantly right is an annoying habit in anyone. Madeleine's so often wrong, bless her. You didn't ask Mother who it was. I thought you would, when she wouldn't tell me."

"She wouldn't have told me, either. And I was not sure if her statement was prompted by instinct or guesswork or knowledge: I think I was unwise in the first place to ask her if she knew. Perhaps you can persuade her that if she knows something we don't, she should go to the police and tell them."

"I'll try. But she may already have done so. Perhaps that's why they let her go off in the dinghy. I do wish she wouldn't take such risks. She's so keen on fishing. She hasn't been here before and I didn't know how poor the fishing would be this year. She brought all her deep sea gear, expecting to have a good time catching the big stuff. A competition takes place here next week. But the fish just aren't around now. The trawlers come in too close and you're lucky if you can even get a snapper some days."

"She showed courage in launching that boat by herself," commented Alan.

"Yes, she's got guts all right, and she's very determined. But she takes risks. She was bathing outside the flags the other day and was quite annoyed when the surf guards had a piece of her for it. And now this! But that constable wasn't as uninterested as she imagined. It was he who told me where she was. I kept watching for her to come in but I missed her in the end. I'm glad someone was decent enough to give her a hand. She was on the beach and had already loaded the boat onto the trailer and started to bring it back when I found her. I suppose someone helped her lift it on."

"It's hard to pull that trailer over the sand," remarked George. "Yes, none of us do it alone by choice. She's strong but she'll strain herself if she does things like that. And she should've asked the boys first before she took their boat. She's not usually so free with other folks' property, but I guess she knew they wouldn't let her go."

"Where were the Harkin men?"

"They're up the bay, all of them, helping a friend clear the gorse from his section. She took advantage of that."

"She said she won't do it again,"

Alan reminded him.

"That's right, so she did. And she won't, either. That's one thing about Mother. She always keeps her word. She's got a thing about being honest, never lying and always saying what she means. But she's so efficient that she wants to run other people's lives for them. And other people's houses too, I'm afraid. I'd better go in and help Madeleine with the vegetables before Mother's had her bath and changed and wants to reorganise everything. She only wants to help but it's a bit frustrating for Maddy at times."

"We shan't keep you," said Jabal. "We need to shower and change too. It was hot on the links today." As they walked back to the cottage, he remarked, "There's a streak of ruthlessness in that woman. I can never understand what pleasure can be derived from watching one of God's creatures dangling in agony at the end of a line in a prolonged struggle for survival."

"She doesn't regard it in that light," said Alan, "just as she doesn't think of the lifeguards when she bathes outside the patrolled zone. It's simply lack of thought, not ruthlessness. She may believe that fish don't feel. Perhaps they don't."

"That's what the slave traders said about negroes. 'They don't feel as we do'. It's on a par with 'The fox enjoys the hunt' and other stupid excuses for inflicting pain and suffering."

"You look really angry, Jabe."

"I am angry. I'm angry that seven people over there are suffering prolonged torture at the end of a police line until one of them will be pulled in. I'm angry when I see Madeleine's dark shadowed eyes, and the look of distress, like that of a hurt child, on Casey's big hairy face, and the earnest frown on William's — the oldest brother, trying to protect his family. I'm angry when Mrs Sayer tries to rid herself of worry by torturing fish, climbing Lion Rock and surfing outside the flags. Poor woman. I should not have been so rude to her. Each is suffering and trying in his or her own way to ease that suffering as best they can. And I'm angry with myself for *being* angry, because *anger resteth in the bosom of fools* and if I were not a fool I'd know by now which of those brothers stabbed Graham Cowan."

"Do you normally know who the guilty person is in — how long has it been? Four days?"

"No, but I don't normally have a maximum of three suspects. This case should be simple and I'm not finding it so. *Why* was the fellow killed? We don't even know that."

"Do you think Mrs Sayer really knows who did it?"

"In a murder enquiry, three-quarters of those involved think they know. It's unwise to say so."

"She spoke with some assurance."

"And little discretion. If she knows, she should go to the police, not tell the next-door neighbours. It's my fault. I should not have asked her."

"Do you think she's in danger?"

"It is never advisable to state in public that A killed B. A is apt to resent it and may seek retaliatory measures."

"None of the brothers was present."

"No, but the remark could be repeated, in all innocence, by her son, and she may already have made the same statement to others in the family. I don't think she's put herself at risk, because of the nature of the crime and the criminal. The attack on Cowan was not planned. It was the result of a sudden outburst of rage. The danger is that fear may now be festering in the culprit's soul, and fear can drive a normal, decent man to unexpected outrages."

"Suppose she approaches the murderer and tells him she knows?"

"That's what I'm afraid of. A sudden fright at the knowledge could incite another outburst of rage, and an attempt to eliminate the new menace to safety. I hope that Bradley will persuade her to go to the police and tell them whatever she knows."

"She was in the kitchen most of that afternoon, remember? The window looks out on the shed and she could very easily have seen which one of them went into it."

"Then why didn't she say so at first? I think it more likely that she's observed or heard or remembered something since the murder, and made a deduction from it."

"Something we've missed?" asked Alan.

"Or something we've also observed and been too slow to interpret correctly."

"Well, she's not likely to tell you, Jabal, after the way you spoke to her. Perhaps George and I could get her aside and question her more tactfully."

"I'd be glad if you would try. Poor woman. I'm sorry for her. But I think I'm more sorry for the killer. He may be suffering worse agonies than any of the others."

"You mean Bruce," said Alan.

"No, he means Casey," said George.

"My turn first with the bathroom," said Jabal, as they walked into the cottage.

9

"I PUT dates in them," said Madeleine.

Jabal took the dish from her hands. "How very nice of you. Come in and wait to see the Canon's eyes light up when we show him."

Madeleine sat down on the couch. "He's a dear old thing, isn't he?"

"He's a fine man. He was a dedicated churchman in his day and although he's enjoying his retirement he's still involved in many charitable and other organisations, rendering very willing and useful help to others."

"Like I said — a dear old thing, where is he?"

"At the moment taking a shower. The archdeacon's out buying our evening meal."

"What will that be?"

"It could be fish and chips or it could

be meat pies. We've left the choice to the archdeacon. The scones will be a very welcome addition to whatever he brings."

"Brad says he was talking to you this morning."

"Yes." Jabal waited hopefully for her to say he had told her his guilty secret, but she made no reference to it. He remarked after a few moments, "He's a pleasant young man."

"I'm glad you like him. We're going to get married at Easter . . . that is, I mean . . . I suppose we are."

"You have doubts?"

"Not about Brad. I adore the silly guy. But if I marry him I get Irma for a mother-in-law. I don't like her and she doesn't like me."

"Why don't you like her?"

"I don't really know. There's nothing actually wrong with her. She's honest and good-looking and active and energetic and willing to help and very fond of Brad and works in a Church shop once a week and — oh,

I don't know. She's awfully neat and tidy. She hates messes or any form of clutter or dust or disorder. She won't let me leave one single dish unwashed, not even a fork. She's always cleaning and polishing and making me feel a slovenly, incompetent housewife. She doesn't think I'm good enough for her son. She's forever tidying the living room and dusting the ledges and organising the kitchen. I should be grateful to her."

"And you're not?"

"No. I don't mind a bit of dust myself or a few books lying around and I prefer to leave the dishes until there's a sinkful. She can't bear that. It's a sort of fetish with her, that everything should be kept clean and tidy. She's so neat herself in her dress, and never a hair out of place. I say, I'm not giving a single valid reason for not liking her, am I? Not a logical reason at all. We just don't seem to click."

"You'd forgo your marriage for a trivial matter like that?"

"It's not trivial. I'd be saddled with her."

"And what does that matter? Good heavens, girl, your situation is far from unusual. Mothers-in-law were thoughtfully provided by the good Lord to act as a whipping post for young brides. You're not supposed to *like* them. They fulfil a need, they serve a purpose, and they can come in handy at times for baby-sitting."

Madeleine laughed. "Well, at least you don't quote Ruth and Naomi to me."

"Certainly not. Have you ever considered why the story of Ruth and Naomi is so well-known and so often told? It's because it provides such a startling exception to the general rule. It is so extraordinary, so unexpected, so contrary to custom, that it qualifies as an historical event. Can you name any other woman in history who wanted to follow her mother-in-law? Have you met any yourself?"

"I know several who tolerate them."

"You can learn to do the same. It will supply a good salutary discipline for the betterment of your immortal soul, a built-in training course which will save you the trouble and expense of attending one of those fashionable seminars which claim, for a substantial fee, to develop your self-assurance, tolerance, and listening skills. Now aren't you fortunate?"

"No," laughed Madeleine. "But I might persuade Brad to go and live in Australia. That would be a simpler solution."

"She could follow. You should tame your dragon, not run from it."

"She's too old to tame. If Ruth was so unusual, what did the other brides do in those days? How did they deal with their mothers-in-law?"

"Much more understandably. Smote them with a sharp sword under the fifth rib."

"I don't think that's necessary for me just yet. Irma does have admirable qualities. She just makes me feel inferior and maybe that's because I *am* inferior." Madeleine's tone grew more serious. "How *can* anyone kill another person? How could anyone stab poor Graham? You must have to hate someone enormously before you could do a terrible thing like that."

"No. It just needs a sudden overflow of emotion, a momentary loss of self-control in a heated argument. That's how it's thought that Cowan was killed."

"Then it wasn't Bradley. Bradley doesn't lose his temper. Nor does Irma. Nor Roma."

"But your brothers do?"

Madeleine nodded. She looked very miserable.

"Madeleine, if you think one of your brothers did it, try to persuade him to go to the police and say so. It would be best for all of you, including him. The police will get their man in the end. They're extremely thorough and a confession would bring about the same end result without subjecting you

157

to more of the harrowing discomfort you're all going through now."

"I know. If I was sure one of them had done it, I'd do my best to persuade him to give himself up. It's affecting everyone, isn't it? Not just our family, either, but the whole bay. Piha will become notorious. It's such a small place but soon everyone will know the name."

"Piha is already well known for many things. The surf life-saving championships."

"And a high record of deaths by drowning."

"I am told that there hasn't been one single fatality among those bathing in the patrolled area."

"But lots along the rest of the beach, and fishermen are swept off rocks and people fall out of boats."

"There's a plant here, they say, that grows nowhere else in the world. *Hebe obtusata*, is it? Or *ipomea palmata*? I can never remember."

"We also stock at least five different

varieties of highly-poisonous berries. A child dies from eating them now and then."

"There are historic remains of the earthworks of an ancient Maori pa."

"Which was captured about 1700 by Kawharu, the chief of the Ngati Whatua tribe. He threw some of the occupants over the cliff, slaughtered others, took a few as slaves, carried off the women and ate the babies."

"That was nearly three hundred years ago. Your bay is also noted for its sunshine, for the Lion, the Camel, the Gap, the Blowhole . . . "

"And crime. It's a good spot for growing cannabis, but that's a mere peccadillo compared with some of the other offences. Some years ago a couple of smart guys stole a body from the Waitumete cemetery, brought it here and put it in an empty bach, then set fire to the bach. One of them beetled off to Australia and the other pretended the body in the bach was his and claimed insurance for him."

"I remember something of that. They were caught, weren't they?"

"Yes. A dentist identified the dental remains of the burnt corpse and knew it wasn't the man who'd been insured and gone off to Australia."

"That shows you how thorough investigations are. The killer of Cowan has no hope of escaping the police net. His best course is to give himself up. You mentioned growing cannabis. Is there much of it here?"

"Yes. All sorts of weirdos come out here and adopt what they call 'alternative life styles', which is generally an excuse to throw off all normal restrictions of decent society. There's so much bush that they make an income by growing plantations of cannabis. It's very profitable. A woman I know of who has a holiday home here arrived one weekend and found a little circle of ground had been cleared in her section and used for a dozen plants. There was even fertiliser spread carefully round them. It must've been someone living in the bay who did it, someone who knew she came seldom and didn't expect her to arrive."

"And what do you think of these people, Madeleine? The cannabis growers?"

"I don't think they realise what harm they're doing. So many believe that cannabis isn't really harmful and that marijuana ought to be legalised. I thought so myself once, until I saw a film on it and read some of the real facts. You can hardly blame them if they don't know. With all this unemployment, it's an easy way to make a living for them."

"So you wouldn't condemn anyone who planted it as a source of income without realising the consequences to others?"

"It would depend. If they really didn't know, I wouldn't blame them, but so many pretend after they're caught that they did it in all innocence, and they're lying. But at least it's not like murder. I still can't believe at times that murder's really happened in our house. There's only horror waiting ahead, isn't there? Someone to be arrested and taken away and put in jail. I think I'll go back now, Mr Jarrett. I shan't wait for Canon Cumbit. But thank you for cheering me up for a little while. It's not your fault I've got all depressed again." She made an effort to smile. "I'll go home now and devise a way to take your advice and stick a sword under Irma's fifth rib."

"That was *not* my advice, young woman."

"I shall plead as defence that a respected vicar put me up to it." She was making a pathetic attempt to look cheerful as Jabal showed her to the door.

Dinner that evening comprised date scones and bacon and egg pie, a fact Alan was proud of, as the Takeaway seldom stocked such a luxury. Clara the cat also approved the choice when she strolled in for her share.

"And now," said George, when the dishes were washed and put away, "we can have a look at the golf book Madeleine lent us. Where is it?"

"We weren't so bad today, though," remarked Alan. "I took only eight on the water hole and Jabal almost did the third in par."

"*Almost*," said Jabal. "Only one over, on a par four. We appeared to have improved simply because the others were a little worse than usual. They're even more out of practice than we are. Cliff Waynes has to manage that huge North Shore parish on his own — not even a curate. It's a wonder he was permitted to take a fortnight's holiday, poor chap."

"Don't start pitying your adversaries. We must be hard and aggressive and merciless. Here's Will's book. *Expert Golf Instruction* by Bob Charles."

"What?" Jabal took the book from him. "So it is! Bob Charles!"

"Bob Charles?" echoed George. "Good gracious!"

"What of it?" asked Alan. "Isn't he any good?"

"He's excellent." Jabal was flicking through the pages. "And I see the photographs and diagrams and explanations are well set out."

"Then what's the matter? It suited Will Harkin all right."

"Yes," said George. "It suited Will Harkin very well. Bob Charles, you ignoramus, is a left-handed golfer."

"Oh! Then Will . . . "

Jabal told him, "Bob Charles was right-handed in most other matters. Listen to this, page 22: 'I cannot see anything odd about playing the ball left-handed. In fact it is 'natural' for me to hit the ball this way and the truth of the matter is that I am otherwise a right-hander. The only time I do things as a southpaw is when I hold an object with both hands, such as a baseball bat or a cricket bat or a golf club'."

"Or a large fish knife," said Alan. "Held with both hands and thrust from left to right."

"There are many people who are partially ambidextrous," said Jabal. "They write their name with the right hand, use a spoon with the right, shave with their right, but when it's a matter of wielding an axe, a golf club — or, as you say, a large knife — they use both hands, the left one being the guide."

"So we're back where we started from," said Alan. "I thought it had been narrowed down to Bruce or Casey."

"I'd now say Casey or Will," said George.

"Have you any good reason for eliminating Bruce?"

"I haven't eliminated him, but I doubt that he did it. He's so worried about his brothers. He asked me yesterday what would happen to one of them if guilty. He was full of concern for them."

"A not uncommon attitude," remarked Jabal, "among those seeking to free themselves from suspicion. Hm . . . I

165

see this preface by Gary Player recommends the book for both right-handed and left-handed players. *Check-points before the hit*. Pass me that two iron, will you, Alan?"

10

"CANON CUMBIT will give you the signal to start," said Jabal, "and you can wave to us the minute you reach the top. Do you always climb in bare feet?"

"My feet are pretty tough and I get a better grip with bare toes. I don't usually have a shirt on, but it's so much colder this morning. The weight of one shirt shouldn't affect the results." Bruce was making an attempt to sound enthusiastic but in spite of his efforts he gave the impression of not caring a brass button whether he broke his record or not.

Alan asked, "Where are all your family? Why aren't they here to cheer you on?"

"It's hardly a national event. I climb the Lion every morning. But I told them you'd offered to time me and

167

they'll be interested in the result. Casey could really beat me hollow if he tried. He just seems to walk straight up with those big strong legs of his. He's never let me time *him* and I think that's because I might be disappointed with my own efforts if I did. He's gone surfing, Will and Brad are going down the beach to dig for tuatuas for one of the Lodge guests who's never tasted them and is keen to do so. Mad's visiting a friend, going to help her paint her kitchen, I think she said, and they want an early start. Irma's fishing."

"Not in the boat again?"

"No, she's not crazy. I think she just took the boat out yesterday to let off steam," said Bruce, with a flash of understanding beyond his years. "She's round in her favourite nook the other side of the Lion, hoping to get fish for lunch. She can see the highest spot from where she fishes so she said she'll watch out for me and cheer when I get to the top. But Roma's coming to watch. She's a good sport. She asked me to wait till she gets here. I'll go over and be ready."

Bruce walked down the beach to the base of the Rock, while Alan, Jabal and George seated themselves on one of the tussocky hillocks facing the sea. It was a bleak, chilly day, and the sky was overcast with dark low clouds, as the wind had changed unexpectedly overnight. George was holding the stopwatch. "The whole Harkin family starts the day early," he observed. "But I think most of the holidaymakers are still in bed." He watched Bruce walk over the black sand. "That poor boy! I think he's feeling the effects of Cowan's killing more than any of the others."

"He will be if he was responsible for it," remarked Jabal.

"How can you suspect *him*? A thoroughly decent, well-brought-up youngster? All right, don't say it. I know your cynical views and if it wasn't him it has to be Casey or

Will. Oh, here's Mrs Pearce."

"I'm sorry I'm late," said Roma. "Have I kept you all waiting? Three more Lodge guests checked out and I had to refund deposits and put their keys away in the flat. The Lodge is more than half-empty now. The police have taken statements and names and addresses and the guests are free to leave, so they're all packing up and going home. There'll be no one left soon. You can't blame them for wanting to get out of it. I wish the rest of us could just run away and leave it all behind us."

"Yes, it's a harrowing experience for you all. Are you going to sit down here with us?"

"I think I might go over to the Rock and watch from the bottom. That'll let Bruce know that I'm interested. I can't see the whole climb from there, but I'll watch him start and then go round the base to where I can see him reach the top. Poor Bruce. It's good of you to encourage him. He's so listless now and he won't eat. He didn't expect to spend his holidays involved in a horrible affair like this."

"It's horrible for all of you," said Jabal, wondering why so many of the household singled out Bruce for sympathy. "Teenagers can often stand a distressing experience such as this better than their elders."

She waved to Bruce. "He's seen me." She started to walk over to the Lion. Bruce was watching her. When she grew near, he signalled his readiness to start. George stood up, his stopwatch in his hand, the other arm raised. Then he dropped his right arm smartly, pressed the watch button and Bruce sprang into action.

They admired the easy movements he made as he climbed rapidly up the rugged right-hand side of the Lion, pulling himself over the projecting outcrops, heaving up with his weight on his arms, pushing with his feet, swinging from side to side as he grasped one hold and then another, springing over the few flat portions. It was obvious that he knew every inch of the route.

Roma had disappeared from view. As the tide was out she had apparently walked round the base to watch from another point. In less than four minutes Bruce was already more than half-way up. Then suddenly, "Something's wrong!" cried Alan. He and Jabal sprang to their feet. Bruce was clutching at part of the cliff with one hand while the other swung loosely at his side. His right foot appeared to be touching solid ground but the left was dangling in the air.

Jabal ran across the sand, Alan close behind him and George following as best he could. As they grew nearer the Lion it was obvious that Bruce was in trouble. "He can't hold, he can't hold." cried Alan. "Can we catch him? Break his fall?"

But Jabal was already climbing the Rock, hastily, clumsily, unfamiliar with the contour and not knowing where to tread or pull or twist. "Hold on, Bruce," he called, but doubted if his voice could be heard above the roar of the sea. Then Bruce momentarily turned his head and saw him. One hand was still clutching a tongue of rock, his right foot was on a small ledge, but he was swaying dangerously as he tried to secure a better grip. At last Jabal was on a shelf below him and just able with his right hand to reach the dangling foot, to take some of Bruce's weight. He avoided looking down at the sharp rocks below, but pressed himself against the side of the cliff and tried to establish a firm footing on the small ledge. He hung on with his left hand, braced himself against the cliff, placed his right hand under Bruce's left foot and pushed up with all his strength. "Up, Bruce. Go up. Now. Put your weight on my hand."

"I can't. I'm coming down." Bruce twisted his head round briefly again. "I'll jump over there, to the left. Can

173

you try to pull me in? I'm coming. I can't hold on."

There was no time to argue. Bruce knew his Lion and Jabal had glimpsed another, wider shelf to his left. Bruce let go with his right hand and with pressure on his right foot threw himself to the left. His feet seemed to fly towards Jabal. One caught him a crippling blow in the mid section, the other landed under his ear. Jabal grasped wildly at the boy's shirt, pulled, and flung himself and Bruce towards the shelf. For a moment he thought they were falling, then it was Bruce who was pressing him against the cliff, steadying him, as he found a footing. The shock of the impact had bruised them both but they were safe. For a few moments neither of them spoke, as they recovered their breath and established their position. Then it was the boy who gave the orders. His face was ashen but his speech under control. "Can you move now, Mr Jarrett? Keep your weight back against the cliff, but turn slowly to the right. See that bit poking out? It's solid rock. If you can get a good hold on it with your right hand you'll be able to lift your left leg and put your knee on that piece below. That's right. Now push with your right hand, hoist yourself up, swing round, climb over that sharp spine . . . "

Jabal was not sure afterwards how either of them had managed it. It must have taken only a few minutes but it seemed an hour before they were at last on the centre track and staggering uncertainly down it. A tourist climbing up gave them a startled look, seemed about to speak and then passed on. Jabal could feel a trickle down his cheek and guessed that they were both displaying flesh wounds.

At the bottom they sank onto the sand. Then Bruce said simply, "Thanks."

Alan and George were beside them. "What happened? Are you all right? You're bleeding."

"We're all right," Jabal assured them,

then turned to the boy. "Why didn't you climb up when I took your weight?" He felt angry that Bruce had chosen to take a course which had endangered the life of them both.

Bruce faced him and he saw there were tears in the boy's eyes. "I couldn't." He held out his left hand. "Look. It's still numb. Someone hit me with a knife handle."

Jabal gazed at the boy's knuckles. The skin had been broken in two places and blood was slowly seeping out.

"I couldn't use both hands," Bruce explained. "I might've just managed to get up using only one, but I thought he might bash at that one too. I suppose he couldn't reach it. It was in a sort of niche with rock each side."

"Hit you?" repeated Alan. "Someone hit you? Who was it?"

"I don't know," said Bruce. "I only saw a hand with the knife handle in it."

"I'll stay with Bruce," said Jabal. "Would you two mind finding his brothers and telling them what's happened?"

"Oh, no, don't do that," said Bruce in alarm. "I'm all right."

"It's not serious, is it?" asked Alan, and then the reason for Jabal's request occurred to him. "Of course. They may have seen you fall, Bruce, so it would be as well to let them know that you're not badly hurt. Come on, George. You go up to the house and I'll look round the beach."

As they hastened off, Jabal turned to the boy. He was white, shaking, but trying to appear unruffled and to speak calmly as he asked, "Did I hurt you much, Mr Jarrett? Landing on you like that?"

"No, of course not."

"Your face is bleeding."

"So is yours. We knocked against the cliff."

"You've got a nasty bash above your eye. And I felt myself kicking you in the neck. Good thing I didn't have shoes on, wasn't it?"

177

"You showed more wisdom that I gave you credit for. It was even more fortunate that you were wearing a shirt."

"Oh yes. You got hold of the material. You couldn't have pulled me in if . . . "

"Don't think about what might have happened. It didn't. Let me see your hand again. Can you move your fingers yet? I don't think any are broken."

"Someone hit me," said the boy. "He *hit* me. He wanted me to fall."

"Are you sure you were deliberately hit, Bruce? Could it have been an accident, a tourist unintentionally dropping a knife?" Jabal knew the foolishness of his question even as he asked it.

"It was done on purpose. I saw a hand holding a knife handle, one of those big white imitation bone ones."

"Had you ever seen it before? Could you recognise it?"

"No. We've got nothing like it at home and I haven't seen anyone on the beach with it. Who'd *do* it, Mr Jarrett? Who would want me to fall down?"

"Do you think someone else fond of climbing wanted to prevent you from breaking a record time up the Rock?"

Bruce shook his head vigorously. "Only a few of the kids in the bay ever climb up this way, and the ones who do know quite well what would happen if you hit someone's hand while it was holding his weight. They wouldn't be so stupid."

"Bruce, have you annoyed anyone? Had an argument with any of the tourists or the residents? Or even the Lodge guests? Offended one of the bach owners? Been cheeky to a gang member? Accused anyone of growing cannabis? Threatened anyone? Think. Think hard."

"I don't need to think. I'd remember if I'd had a row with anyone in the bay. Graham was the only person I quarrelled with. I've spent nearly all my holidays with my family so I haven't seen much of other people. Just a game of tennis now and then or surfing with some of the regulars who come over. Talking to people in the store, or ones we know that come to see us . . . no, honest. I can't think of anyone who'd have it in for me."

"You said you saw a hand holding the knife. Could you see if there was a sheath on the knife?"

"I think the hand held the handle. It was just the end of the handle that came down on my fingers, but I got the impression it was fairly long. Say six inches or so. It all happened so quickly that I can't be sure."

"What was the hand like? Old? Young? Smooth? Rough? Any marks you could recognise it by if you saw it again?"

"Sorry, no. As I said, it was all too quick. But I caught a glimpse of a gold ring."

"Which of your brothers wears a ring?"

"My brothers? What do you mean?"

There was a note of horrified indignation in Bruce's voice.

Jabal realised he had spoken too hastily. His head was aching and his mind not functioning as clearly as he could wish. He said quickly, "Everyone knew you were going to climb the Rock this morning at eight o'clock. Someone might have put a ring on his finger to make his hand look like the hand of one of your brothers — that is, if one of your brothers wears a ring." What nonsense he was talking. He hoped the dazed condition of the boy would allow him to accept this stupid suggestion.

It worked. Bruce's anger subsided. "Oh, I see. Yes. Just for a moment I thought you suspected Boxer or Will. Yes, Boxer wears a signet ring. Will has one too but he doesn't often wear it now. They were both twenty-first birthday presents."

"Would you be able to recognise the ring?"

"Not a hope. It was just a flash of gold."

"Could you tell which hand was holding the knife? Left or right? Try to remember what you saw. Did you see the thumb? Was it like this? Or this?" Jabal closed each fist round a pebble.

"I don't know. What does it matter? Yes, I saw a thumb. I remember now."

"And did the hand come from your left or your right? Please think, Bruce. Try to visualise it. If you can get it clear now I shan't ask you again."

Bruce closed his eyes. Then opened them and said, "The hand came from the left. The person holding the knife could only have been on my left. There wasn't room for anyone on the other side. He must have struck from the left, and he couldn't reach my right hand because the rock was protecting it. He hit my left hand twice and I saw the flash of a ring when the knife went up the second time."

"Thank you. That's a big help. Are you fit to go home now?"

"Yes, of course." Bruce slowly flexed his injured fingers. "I can move them easily now." He rose unsteadily to his feet.

Jabal got up too. "Suppose you come to the cottage first and clean up there?"

"Oh, thanks. That's a good idea, just in case Mad's come home. I don't want to go in looking like this. She'd worry and fuss."

Bruce was still in the bathroom of the cottage and Jabal was making coffee when George and Alan came in. "Casey was swimming," said Alan. "His surf board had been left on the beach. Will and Bradley were fairly near the Lion, both to the right of it, but in different places. Roma was round the base, near one of the Fingers. None of them knew anything had happened. All right, don't look like that. None of them *admitted* knowing anything had happened. They *seemed* surprised. Roma was wondering why Bruce hadn't appeared at the top but she thought — sorry, she *said* she thought that she hadn't been looking at the right time and had simply missed him before he went down again. I didn't tell them what had happened. I said Bruce had not completed the climb because one of his hands was bruised and he'd put it off until another time. But I told Roma Pearce a little bit more. I said he'd had a slight accident and asked her to go and tell Inspector Chambers that there had been a disturbing incident on the Rock."

"Oh, good work, Alan. Trevor'll guess it's something that needs his urgent attention."

"Are you hurt, Jabe?"

"No. Bruised and shaken. I thought we were both done for."

"Was he really hit, or did he imagine it?"

"He's convinced someone hit his knuckles with a knife handle, in order to make him fall. It's lucky he's so familiar with that side of the Lion. We'd both have fallen otherwise. It was a near thing. Is Madeleine back yet?"

"There was no one in the house," George told him. "I looked round the section and saw only a constable there. If Madeleine's helping a friend paint the kitchen, she'll probably be away all morning."

Roma arrived while they were all drinking coffee. Bruce was quiet and composed but very pale. "I guessed you'd be here, Bruce. What's this about an accident? Are you OK?"

"Yes, fine. But I wouldn't be, if it hadn't been for Mr Jarrett."

"I've told Inspector Chambers and he's going to talk to you."

"Whatever for? Why did you go and tell *him*?"

"I asked her to," said Alan.

"Any accidents on the Lion have to be reported to the police," lied Roma. "Statistics and so on."

"Is that something new they've brought in? Oh well, I suppose it's a good idea. I think I'll go home now before Mad gets back. I don't want anyone to tell her first and upset her, so I'd like to be there when she arrives. I'll change my shirt before she sees me. I must look a mess."

"You've plenty of time," said Roma. "I'll come back with you. I might even wash that blood-stained shirt if you're good."

They had been gone only a few minutes when Trevor Chambers arrived. "I've put a cordon round the Rock and I've phoned a request for more men to be sent out. I don't imagine you sent Mrs Pearce to me to report a mere accident. What happened? What's that cut above your eye, Jabe? Are you all right?"

Jabal gave him a brief account. " . . . and the boy claims that he was hit over the knuckles with the handle of a knife. He's gone back to the house."

"Yes, I saw him go in. I thought I'd get the story from you before I talk to him. I'll let the kid get over his shock for a bit. My men will round up everyone on the beach. It's a good thing it's such a dull morning. There's hardly anyone in the water and only a few on the Rock. Let's hope one of the climbers saw what happened. I don't like this, Jabal."

"No. If what the boy said is true, it was a deliberate attack, a planned attempt to kill him, unlike the stabbing of Cowan, which was done in a fit of rage."

"Exactly. It could possibly have been some silly lout who'd climbed up and thought it funny to rap some knuckles which he saw appear over a ledge of rock. Violence for the sake of violence. There's plenty of it around."

"But you don't believe that, do you?"

"No. That type carry flick knives or home-made weapons, not large bone handled blades."

"Bruce didn't recognise the knife. He couldn't see the hand clearly enough to guess the age or sex of the owner. But he did see a flash of a gold ring. The hand came from the left of him and he saw the thumb as it clutched the handle, so it appears that the striker was using his left hand."

"Indeed? Well, we'll question everyone who was on, or near, the Lion. We'll squeeze the truth out of any lout. But it seems more probable that whoever killed Cowan thought young Bruce was on to him and got the wind up."

"One or two of the household suspected that Bruce knew more than he admitted about Cowan's death. But this was a vicious attack. It doesn't fit with the murder of Cowan and may not have been done by the same person. Anyone could have found out the time that Bruce intended to start his climb. The attacker would have to be up the Lion in position before he arrived at that spot."

"Which of the brothers could've done that?"

"Either. They were out of sight when the climb started. Bruce mentioned the other day that Casey can climb the Rock faster than he can, and Casey was in the sea when Alan found him. *Without* his surf board. He'd left that on the beach. But Will was also handy and there are so many ways up that Rock that he could've scrambled up unseen before Bruce started to climb. Can you get the boy to hospital, Trevor?"

The Inspector nodded. "Yes. A very sensible suggestion. I'll arrange it now. Then I'd like to go over to the Rock. Are you fit to come over and show me just where it happened, Jabe?"

"Yes, certainly."

"Do you want us to keep quiet about this?" asked Alan.

"No, I don't. You can tell the world." Trevor's face darkened. "Whoever it was, he's not going to get away with it. I'll hunt him down if it takes me all year. You saved that kid, Jabe. You could both have been killed. It must've been a frightening experience."

"It was," said Jabal. *"Fear came upon me and trembling, which made all my bones to shake. It was the boy's skill and knowledge of the Lion*

189

which saved us both. *My feet were almost gone, my steps had well nigh slipped.*"

"Hm," said Alan. "He's recovered."

"Obviously," agreed Inspector Chambers. "He's back to abnormal."

11

"I TRUST you had an enjoyable game of golf?" enquired Trevor that evening.

"I detect a note of bitterness in your voice, Trevor. Yes, we did, thank you. I gather you haven't had a joyous time yourself?"

"I have not. We acted smartly and no cars left the beach before we'd rounded up and interviewed everyone who was out and about. Most of the holidaymakers were still in bed, owing to the cold weather, but that wasn't really a stroke of luck for us. It reduced our work, but if more had been on the Lion, the attack on the boy might not have taken place. Two persons were having an early dip and three climbing. None of them saw anything amiss except one climber who reports passing a man and a boy who were dripping blood and had evidently been fighting."

"We were in a bit of a mess," said Jabal.

Alan said, "His black eye caused a sensation on the links. We were accused of squabbling over who does the dishes. How is Bruce?"

"He's quite all right, but we're no further ahead in discovering who hit him. We gathered all the rest of the Harkin household together in their living-room and paraded the five holidaymakers who'd been on the beach. The Harkins thought they were being asked to recognise the strangers. The strangers had actually been asked if they'd seen any of the household on or near the Rock that morning. No results either way. Bradley and Will had been seen by one or two, but not on the Lion."

"Where were all the family at the time of the accident? Any alibis?"

"Not a one, not even for the girl, Madeleine, because she and her friend

192

are very vague as to the time she arrived at her friend's house. She says she strolled up slowly and met no one on the way. She'd have had time to shin up the Lion first. As for the others — " The Inspector pulled a piece of paper from his pocket. "Here we are. Casey Harkin surfing. Seen once by Mrs Sayer, who was fishing, and several times by Bradley Sayer and Will Harkin, who were both digging for tuatuas on different parts of the beach."

"When I found Casey," Alan said, "he was swimming beyond the waves. His surf board was on the beach. I beckoned to him and he came in."

"He'd naturally have to leave his surf board on the beach if he intended to climb up the Rock and push his young brother off. Now the others — Irma Sayer was fishing from the other side of the Lion. Says she kept looking up to the summit after eight o'clock to see if Bruce was there. Saw Casey once, but no one else. We checked on that, and she couldn't see much from where she fishes. The rocks project each side of the spot where she sits. Roma Pearce was a short distance round the base of the Lion. Says she got a good view of the start of the boy's climb, then moved on and could not see the place where he had the accident. Did not see you run over to the Rock, Jabal, or climb up, because she had by then gone further round to where she could see Bruce reach the summit. Sounds reasonable. We walked round to test her story and I think she's telling the truth. At least, her account of what one can see from various parts of the base appears to be accurate. That doesn't mean she didn't dash up the Rock and rap the kid's fingers herself."

"There are so many ways up the Rock," said Jabal. "Anyone could have climbed up and down unseen and be well away by the time Bruce and I had reached the bottom. It was slow work making our way round to the centre track — for me, because I'm no climber and didn't know the way, and for Bruce, because he had to guide me, and was hurt and dazed himself. We were neither of us bounding with energy when we found the track and we took our time walking down."

"There are several possibilities. First, the whole thing could be a fake, an attempt by the boy, if he killed Cowan, to put us off the scent. But that would demand a quality of acting I doubt if he possesses."

"I agree."

"Then the attack could've been made by a stranger who got away before we searched. That's unlikely. I think Will Harkin or Sayer would've seen anyone running across the sand. The five who admit to being on the beach seem innocuous enough. A middle-aged couple in the water, another younger couple climbing, and the fifth, the one you startled, is a pensioner who comes here each year to stay with his married daughter and her family, who live in the bay. I can't see any of them being implicated. Then it could have been done by a resident, a bach owner or a Lodge guest, but why? For some personal reason we don't yet know of? Or did some eccentric guess that Bruce had killed Cowan and decide to mete out justice? There again, how did they manage to get away without being seen? Of course we'll question everyone in the bay."

"I asked the boy if he had had a disagreement with anyone in the district and he denied it."

"Yes, and it would be a foolish way to attack him. No one knows that Cowan named the brothers before he died, so it's unlikely that anyone would attack Bruce for a personal reason in the hope that this crime would also be attributed to Cowan's killer. In fact, there would be more risk that a person suspected of this would have Cowan's murder pinned on him too."

"But it must be known that only the members of the Harkin household are suspected of killing Cowan. It would be natural for them to tell their friends, and the story would soon get round."

"Providing a scapegoat for the attack on Bruce? It's possible, I suppose. But it's far more likely that one of the household tried to get rid of the kid. And that means one of his two brothers. Mrs Pearce says that Bruce announced at the dinner table last night that he knew who'd killed Cowan. He hinted that he'd heard or witnessed something of importance, but he wouldn't answer any of their questions and in the end he refused to discuss it any more."

"What does the boy say about it?"

"Unfortunately she told me that after I'd packed him off to hospital. I'll ask him when I go in."

"I think he would have been bluffing," said Jabal. "He told me that he knew which one would not be willing to own up and he based his suspicions on that. He was not in possession of any facts."

"Apparently someone thought he was, knew he was to climb the Rock this morning and decided to stop him from telling what he knew. And that means Will or Casey."

"Any trace of the knife?"

"No. The boy described the handle as large, white, probably imitation bone. Irma Sayer had a black-handled knife in her kit, one belonging to the Harkins and normally kept in the shed. Will Harkin had a blue-handled pocket knife, about four inches long, Bradley Sayer a small brown-handled straight blade, also from the stock in the shed. Casey naturally had none. He was in bathing trunks. Roma Pearce had none. But they all had time to get rid of a knife before we questioned them. It could still be up on the Rock somewhere. Two of us have been up but we couldn't get round to the spot you pointed out, Jabe. We'd have broken our necks."

"I doubt if you'd have found the knife if you'd got there. It'll have been thrown in the sea and covered with sand by now."

"Of course. We'll search the Lion again, just for the record, but I don't expect to find anything useful."

"Did anyone recognise the description of the knife?"

"No. Both William and Casey say there was no such knife on their property, nothing like it in the shed, garage, or anywhere in the house. It would pay one of them to say so, but would they both lie? The girl said the same. We questioned each separately and the answer came readily. Nothing like it, they said. The only large knife they had in the shed was the one used to stab Cowan. A breadknife and a carving knife inside, still there. Don't answer the description."

"It could have been bought at the store."

"We enquired. They don't sell knives."

"You have been thorough. Perhaps it belongs to a Lodge guest or a resident and was found on the beach by one of the brothers."

Alan asked, "Why wasn't the blade

199

of the knife used instead of the handle? Surely that would have been more effective?"

"Knife cuts would be obvious on a dead body," the Inspector explained. "Bruises from a heavy handle could be mistaken for the effect of a knock or a heavy stone landing on the fingers. An attack could not be proved. Whoever did it hoped that it would pass as an accident, when the boy was not alive to give any account."

"Why not kick his hand?" suggested Canon Cumbit. "If I wanted to stop someone from climbing up I think I'd stamp hard on his fingers."

Jabal smiled. "I doubt if you've had enough experience in that field to know what you'd do." He tried to envisage his gentle, elderly friend stamping on someone's fingers, but his imagination was not equal to the task.

"I doubt if any foot could touch the spot," said Trevor. "From what we could see today, one would have to kneel down, or even lie down, to reach the place where the boy's hand was, and could approach only from the left of the boy — that is, the left of the Lion as viewed from the shore. This means, as you pointed out, that the thumb would show if the left hand were used. We've been experimenting. The boy said he saw no sheath. The handle was apparently large enough to be held and used as a weapon."

"What about the ring?"

"Casey was wearing one. Will was not, but he could've taken it off. Bruce was talking to his brothers before we questioned them — they both went up to the house to see what had been going on — and no doubt he mentioned the ring. He has no suspicion of his brothers."

"Yet he was quite realistic about the possibility of their killing Cowan."

"Oh yes, he admitted that even to us. But we can't say that the person who killed Cowan was the same person who attacked Bruce. It was a different sort of crime."

"That's true," agreed Jabal, "but fear of discovery can twist the soul of any man and goad him into acts he would normally shrink from. I feel there's only one person behind this and that must be one of the brothers because of Cowan's dying statement."

"Look, let's go back to that for a minute," said Trevor. "I don't doubt you heard what you did, but have you considered the possibility of Cowan deliberately saying it in order to deceive you? To protect someone else?"

"I don't think he was sufficiently altruistic for that. He might make such an effort for Madeleine, perhaps. Even a scoundrel will sometimes try to protect the woman he loves."

"She wears an engagement ring," observed Trevor, "and she disliked Cowan, even hated him enough to kill him."

"I don't believe it," protested George. "That nice young girl!"

Jabal looked at him sadly. "Even nice young girls, who make date scones for retired canons, can stab men at times."

"That could be why the boy didn't talk," said Trevor. "He's devoted to his sister. And she could very well be the one he knew would not own up. It's harder for a woman to take such a step. Madeleine hasn't had the same opportunities as her brothers to develop strength of character. The men protect her."

"It's logical," said Jabal, "but there's one thing wrong with that theory. Cowan said it was her brother who stabbed him. If he wanted to shield her, he would not have named one of them."

"He said it, but he might not have meant it," argued George.

"He meant it," said Jabal. "You've been present at as many death-beds as I have. It's not a time for false accusations or lying."

"He's right, George," put in Alan. "You know it. I can understand his saying something to protect Madeleine, but not at the expense of one of her brothers. One fact is inescapable — the killer of Cowan was Bruce, Casey or William."

"How did Casey and Will react to the news?" asked Jabal.

"Bruce had seen them before I did, but they were still very angry, or pretending to be, when I spoke to them."

"I think it would be genuine anger in each case, either anger that someone else had tried to kill Bruce, or anger that his own attempt had failed."

Alan suggested, "Irma Sayer could've climbed up and done it. She often climbs over from that side if she's caught by the tide, and no one would see her."

"She could, but why would she? She didn't kill Cowan, so she had nothing to kill Bruce for. She wouldn't attack him to protect one of Madeleine's brothers."

"She might kill to protect her son."

"Her son didn't need protection,

because *he* didn't kill Cowan."

"We're going round in circles," groaned the Inspector. "It seemed such a simple case to start with. One of the three brothers killed Cowan, there's no doubt of that, but we can't be sure the same one attacked Bruce. I don't suppose it was meant merely to frighten him, as a warning?"

"No," said Jabal. "It was an attempt to kill the boy. Unless . . . "

"Unless what?"

"I was thinking of your first suggestion that the whole thing was a fakc. I've known cases where a man thinking himself to be under suspicion has staged an attempt on his own life. It's not uncommon."

George shook his head. "Jabal, you have the most wicked mind! Even if the boy had such an incredible notion, he wouldn't choose that way to pretend an attack on himself."

"Why not? An unexpected fall would be fatal, but a calculated drop at the right time in the right place   onc chosen by himself — would not be unduly risky. He knows every nook and foothold of the Lion. He had one foot anchored when we first saw him in what seemed then to be difficulties, and that foot was still touching firm ground when I reached him. The tip of it, certainly, but it was taking much of his weight. He knew we were watching. He would jump on to a ledge, slide, skip safely down, then limp over to us with a few bruises and tell his story. A good plan."

"Which didn't work because you once won the hundred yards sprint at University," said Trevor. "You got there before he could make his planned jump. You scotched his plan and landed him as well as yourself in genuine trouble. No wonder he was so upset."

"I don't believe it!" protested George indignantly. "You can carry suspicion too far. What about that blow on his hand?"

"Self-inflicted before the climb,"

suggested Jabal. "I watched him climbing but we were some distance away and although he appeared to be using that hand as much as the other, he may have placed it in position but not let it take any pressure. If he killed Cowan it could've been a scheme to put the blame elsewhere."

"On Mrs Sayer, for instance," said Alan. "Then why didn't he just say he'd seen her hit his hand?"

"Because it would have been too obvious that he was naming a scapegoat. She would have denied it and she has a reputation for being truthful."

"Those tears were genuine. Boys that age don't weep readily."

"Unless they are acting. He managed to squeeze a few out — after all, he *had* nearly fallen and he hadn't expected that. Then he put his head down because no more would come. It's not easy to weep at will."

"Oh, you're impossible, Jabal."

George said mildly, "I really don't think it likely. Mr Chambers said earlier that it would take very good acting, better than the boy is capable of. Are you going to grill the poor lad, Inspector?"

"Not for the moment. I've sent him to hospital by ambulance."

"Does he really need hospital treatment? I didn't think his injuries were as bad as that."

"They're not. But he needs protection from further attacks," Trevor explained. "Or else another person needs protection from him. In either case, he's better there. He protested vigorously against going, so I told him it would be a wise precaution to have his hand X-rayed. I may have mentioned the wealth of sport one can indulge in at University and the frustration if an injury, unattended to, prevents full participation. That persuaded him. They'll keep him a couple of days, at my request, and they *will* X-ray his hand, as a matter of routine."

"Do you mind if we discuss it all with the family?" asked Jabal.

"Mind? I'm begging you to. I'm getting nowhere myself. I can't pin it down to any one of the three. I think it may be time to tell them what Cowan said. For several reasons I've hesitated to do so as yet. Well, I'll question the whole lot tomorrow and the Lodge guests too. *Someone* must have seen *something*. Please do your best, Jabal."

The Inspector left and Alan turned to Jabal. "Well, who was it?"

"I don't know. I'm completely baffled."

"Can we assume that the same person killed Cowan and attacked Bruce?"

"Providing Bruce didn't fake his own accident, that's the most likely possibility."

"And you said that the most likely explanation of a thing is nearly always the correct one."

"Yes, nearly always, but not invariably so."

"You also said the most likely suspect is usually the offender."

"Yes, but again, not invariably so."

"You can't wriggle out of it like that. Which of these brothers is the most likely?"

"I don't know."

"Oh, come on, Jabe. Be a bit more helpful. I thought you just had to sum up people and then judge which one is guilty?"

"I made no such claim," protested Jabal. "You were listening to Trevor. But the character of everyone connected with the case is of the utmost importance, not just that of the suspects, but of all who are in any way involved. Each person's personality has an impact on that of others, and the presence of one individual in a group can lead to violence among the rest. He can appear to be an uninterested outsider, yet act as a catalyst to cause reactions."

"Does that apply here?" asked Alan. "Give us your opinion of them all."

"What's your own opinion?" asked Jabal. "You're just as capable as I am of judging them. *You* do a little summing up. *You* examine the personalities involved. Here, take a piece of paper each. Now jot down your impressions of each member of the household. I'll do the same and we can then compare our views. No one can accurately be described in a few words, but general impressions can be helpful."

"I don't see what good it'll do," said Alan, "but I'll try. You do it too, George."

After a few minutes they compared papers. "There's a marked similarity in our opinions," said Jabal. "We've used different adjectives, but we seem to mean much the same. What have we said? Madeleine — open, friendly, naive, careless, affectionate, loyal. Mrs Sayer — forthright, honest, tidy, neat, methodical, efficient, bossy. I've added 'cruel' but you two haven't. One of you put 'courageous' and I think I'd agree with that, too. Casey — bluff, strong, bad tempered, energetic, fond of his sister. Will — much the same. Hardworking, earnest, fond of his sister.

Roma — reliable, industrious, honest, affable, loyal to the Harkins. Bradley — quiet, thoughtful, placid, earnest, self-controlled. Well that's our joint opinion."

"And has anything useful come of it?"

"There are two points of interest," said Jabal. "Firstly, each of us has omitted Bruce from the list."

"Oh, I completely overlooked him," said Alan.

"So did I," said George. "I just forgot. I suppose we none of us seriously consider that he staged that fall himself. What was the second point, Jabe?"

"We all seem to stress family loyalty and affection."

"And what does that indicate?" asked Alan. "Where has it got us? We're no further ahead. Bruce, Casey or Will? We might just as well shuffle their names in a hat."

Jabal slowly crumpled up the papers. "I'd like to know how Madeleine is

212

now. Shall we return her dish?"

"You two can go," said George. "I don't think a visit from the three of us will help and I resign from your team of sleuths. I never did like those restaurants where you examine fish in an aquarium before you pick one out for your dinner."

12

"HERE'S the bowl you brought the scones in, Madeleine."

"You didn't need to fill it with Californian grapes," said Madeleine. "I happen to know what they cost at the store. Thank you very much."

"That was the canon's idea," Alan told her. "I'd suspect attempted bribery if I were you. He went off to golf this afternoon full of scone and purring like Clara."

"He shall certainly have some more. How did you get on with the golf book? Was it any use?"

"We're still studying it," said Jabal. "I hadn't realised that Will was a left-hand golfer."

"Yes. He uses an axe left-hand, too, but he's right-handed in most things. Our father was the same. Was that book just for left-hand players?"

"No, the advice applies to any golfer and it will be very useful to us. Did Will mind your lending it?"

"Of course not. Why should he?" Madeleine looked really surprised at the question. "I hope it will help you. When do you think Bruce will be allowed to come home? Will's wondering whether we should go in and see him this evening."

"I don't think that's necessary," said Jabal. "He was taken to hospital merely as a precaution. He suffered some shock and it's as well to have his hand X-rayed. He'll be discharged shortly." All of which was true, he told himself. Sending Bruce away *had* been a precaution, he *did* incur mild shock and they *would* X-ray his hand, but it was not the whole truth and he felt uncomfortably guilty at deceiving her.

"The Inspector says someone hit him to make him fall, but I just can't believe that. Everyone round here likes Bruce. I think that the person who hit him did it for a joke and couldn't have known that a tap on his fingers would make him let go. But Boxer says anyone, even a child, would be aware that it would loosen his grip and cause him to fall and be killed. He's absolutely furious."

Because Bruce fell or because he didn't? wondered Jabal. He asked, "And how is William taking it?"

"He can't understand why they've taken Bruce to hospital. He says he felt his hand and he's sure nothing was broken. He thinks, as I do, that it could've been a poor attempt at a practical joke by someone who knew no better. He's not too worried about it. But Casey's hopping mad. I've seldom seen him so angry. He tore through here a few minutes ago. He'd picked up some fleas from the cat and he was in a raging temper. He said he was going to go through every room of the Lodge, whether occupied or not, and hunt for a white bone-handled knife."

"He won't find it."

"I know that, but I couldn't stop

216

him." She started to cry. "Excuse me please." She wiped her eyes. "I should be used to the Harkin temper by now. I've grown up with it and I've got my fair share of it myself. It's just that everything's getting me down and knowing Bruce was hurt, and Casey storming out like that, it was all rather upsetting. He quite frightened me. I hope he doesn't do anything silly. There aren't many guests left now in the Lodge and I bet he scares off the few who are still there."

"Are you afraid he'll attack one of them?"

"If he finds a white knife, I know he will. If he doesn't he'll cool down. His rages don't last long. They go as quickly as they come."

She was proved right. In a few minutes Casey returned, calm and a little shamefaced. "It's not there," he told his sister, "or else it's well hidden. Sorry I shouted at you. Good God, have you been crying? Oh, I *am* sorry, Mad. I'm a brute."

Jabal and Alan discreetly left them.

"I didn't know you got fleas from a cat," remarked Alan, as they walked back to the cottage.

"Of course cats have fleas. Haven't you seen the television ads for flea collars?"

"They have them, I know that, but you don't usually get them off cats, as you can off dogs. No wonder the poor fellow was angry. I had one once under my cassock when I was giving communion. I'd been patting a parishioner's over-friendly Labrador. Do you think big dogs have the larger fleas? It was most uncomfortable, I assure you. Poor Casey'll have to wash all his clothes. Or perhaps he'll leave them on and go for a swim to drown all the fleas. He appears to like swimming."

"He's a strong swimmer. I like watching his stroke."

"He's strong altogether. It wouldn't be much of a problem for him to drive a knife into another man's chest. It must be him, Jabe, not Will. Don't you agree?"

"I tell you I don't know."

"Though it's difficult to think of him trying to make his young brother fall down the Rock. I can't help liking the fellow, Jabe."

"Mr Jarrett!" Irma Sayer came out of the shed and hurried over to them. "Have you heard how Bruce is? Why did they take him to hospital? What's happened? They say someone hit him on the fingers while he was climbing the Rock this morning and made him fall. Is that really true?" She looked unusually distraught.

"Yes. You were fishing below, weren't you, Mrs Sayer? Did you see anyone who might have been climbing up to do it?"

"No. The police asked me that. I saw Casey once, in the sea, but no one else. I kept looking up at the summit because Bruce said he was being timed, but he didn't appear. I thought he'd just postponed the climb because it was such a dull day. Then one of the police came round and told me what had happened. But they said he was all right and now he's gone to hospital. I wish they would tell us the truth."

"You were told the truth, Mrs Sayer. Bruce's hand will be X-rayed but it's not thought that it's seriously injured."

"Do you know who hurt him?"

"No, do you?"

She stared at him oddly and he continued, "Mrs Sayer, you told me once that you knew who stabbed Cowan. Do you know who attacked Bruce?"

"I should not have made such a statement, Reverend. I suppose I was upset at the time and spoke without thinking."

"But you did make it and I believe you meant it. Do you also know who hit Bruce's fingers?"

"I tell you, I saw no one."

"But can you guess? Have you an idea based on something we don't know about?"

"If I have, I don't intend to broadcast the fact." Her lips curled into the curious half-smile he had seen on her before.

"You would be wise not to," he said. "But I do urge you to go to the police and tell them what it is you know. Bruce also hinted, remember, that he knew Cowan's killer, and the next morning he had an accident and was nearly killed."

"You think someone hit him to make him fall down the cliff? I suppose you're right. He's a strong, skilled climber. He goes up the Lion every morning."

"Have you told anyone else that you think you know who killed Graham Cowan?"

Her face showed slight alarm. "I might have."

"Then go to the police and tell them your suspicions, or you may be in danger yourself."

"I'll think about it." She was frowning as she moved back towards the shed.

"Does she know?" asked Alan.

"She's probably guessed who stabbed Cowan. She must know the family well by now and she was in the kitchen that afternoon, where the window looks onto the shed. She says she saw no one go in there but she may be keeping quiet because she doesn't want her son to marry into the family of a convicted murderer and hopes the case will never be solved, not so much out of consideration for the killer as for the good name of her future in-laws."

"But she wouldn't condone hurting the boy."

"No. She could be prepared to overlook a killing in a burst of sudden rage, under provocation, but she's upset over Bruce. She may talk to the police now. I certainly hope so. She doesn't scare easily and may be too confident of her ability to look after herself."

"Bruce told the whole family he would start the climb at eight. She was out fishing before that. She could have climbed up herself and bashed his hand."

"That's true," agreed Jabal. "She was in a good position to do so. But she had no reason to. She had nothing to fear from Bruce because she didn't kill Cowan herself and she wouldn't go to such lengths to prevent him from accusing, or giving away, one of his brothers. If Bruce himself is the killer, she would not be interested enough to attack him in revenge, or appoint herself judge and executioner. I can see no reason for anyone other than Cowan's murderer to attack the boy. As Trevor said, we're going round in circles and getting nowhere."

Nevertheless, they continued to discuss the matter over the evening meal. "You've talked a lot to all three of them," said George. "You said that people give themselves away."

"So they do, in time."

"Hasn't there been time yet? I'm disappointed in you as a detective,

Jabe. Shouldn't you be making clever deductions or listing significant facts?"

"Significant facts have emerged all right but I'm a bit slow at the clever deductions. I'm too dull to interpret correctly the facts that we know and the indications that are so contradictory."

"What indications? Are there any that Alan and I haven't noticed for ourselves?"

"There are one or two interesting points . . . "

"Hold on," said Alan. "I want to write them down. All right, I'm ready. List your interesting points."

Jabal thought for a moment and then said, "Very well. One — Bruce Harkin told us he'd go straight to the police if he had any evidence or proof to offer them."

"And he didn't, so you mean that when he said at the dinner table that he knew who did it, he was merely bluffing?"

"He probably was, but that's not what I meant. Two — Mrs Sayer is a keen fisherwoman."

"Ah — I get it. She was so intent on her fishing when Bruce was being attacked that she would not have seen anyone climb up so someone could have gone round that way?"

"Perhaps, but that's not what I had in mind. Three — there is a sink in the Harkins' shed."

"So the murderer washed the blood off his hands?"

"I doubt if there was any blood on them. I don't think he went anywhere near the sink. But there *is* one there."

"Oh, that is significant, isn't it, George?" said Alan with sarcasm. "Of course it changes the whole aspect of the case."

"There's a sink in my garage at home," remarked George.

"And you lie awake at night obsessed with its deep significance. Can't you do better than that, Jabe?"

"They happen to be puzzling factors."

"Indicating the identity of the murderer?"

"Indicating the guilt of someone whom I know for a fact to be innocent."

"That doesn't make sense."

"Nothing makes sense in this affair."

13

THE following morning was sunny again. At an early hour cars began to arrive at Piha. Surf boards, picnic baskets, children and sun umbrellas were unloaded and the beach was soon alive with noise and activity. The police guard had been removed from the Lion, the Surf Club verandah was manned by the lifeguards on duty and the scene appeared that of a normal summer day. One or two of the holidaymakers pointed out the Harkin house and the Lodge but without much interest. That was the place — that one over there — pass the suntan lotion, please. Violence is too common now to cause a sensation to those not intimately involved. To the visitors, this was just another murder.

"It was Bruce," announced the archdeacon at breakfast. "I worked it all out during the night. He was the one who disliked Cowan the most. He's admitted it. And you said the most likely person, Jabe . . . well, you know what you said. I've seen the significant point about the sink in the shed. Bruce and Casey were painting the boat. Bruce got paint on his hands, and went into the shed to wash if off there. The turpentine would be kept there, too. Graham Cowan was at the sink — he'd been working on his car and gone in to clean his hands, and the boy said 'Get out of the way' or 'What — you here again?' or something equally provocative. Cowan didn't like the boy and took the opportunity to sneer at him or tell him off. Boys of that age are easily offended. They quarrelled bitterly and then Bruce picked up the knife. Of *course* he said he'd give evidence to the police if he had any. That was another of your significant points. He was simply trying to avoid being blamed for the murder. He staged that fall down the cliff because he thought the police were on his scent. Criminals do that. Their guilty conscience makes them imagine everyone suspects them."

"Not in my experience," said Jabal. "They usually have a measure of conceit, which grows as time goes by. They become over-confident that they've got away with their crime."

"Ah, but this was a teenager, remember. Uncertain of himself, lacking assurance, racked by remorse and guilt. They won't be too hard on him, will they? I was so relieved when I realised it was him. It was distressing to think of someone trying to make him fall down the cliff. And of course no one did. He was going to jump, as one of you suggested."

"Oh no, no," said Canon Cumbit, shaking his head. "You've got it all wrong, Alan. I worked it out in the night, too, and it was definitely Casey. I saw the point about the sink, too. Washing the brushes. But Casey would do that. He wouldn't have trusted the boy with the painting. And he was the one best able to use his left hand. When you're lying under a car reaching out with your left hand to unscrew a nut, you develop the ability to control it. And Casey has the fiercest temper. I've eliminated Will, as he has his under command these days. Casey was nearest to the Lion when Bruce was climbing. He went up with no intention of striking the boy but Bruce knew he'd killed Cowan and accused him."

"A strange time to choose," observed Jabal. "Halfway up a difficult rock climb."

George ignored this. "Casey simply lost his temper again. 'How dare you say a thing like that to me?' Rapped him without thinking on the knuckles."

"With a knife he just happened to have taken up with him?"

"No, with a knife he found there. That's why no one recognised it. It'd been dropped by some tourist one day. Casey noticed it in his rage and picked it up to hit the boy's hand. He didn't mean any harm."

"I don't agree," said Alan. "Why would he suddenly leave his swim to climb up the Rock?"

"To encourage his brother. He only became enraged when Bruce accused him of the murder. Don't you think that's right, Jabal?"

"I keep telling you, I have no idea which of the three killed Cowan. I'm utterly confused and puzzled."

"We were right about the sink, were we? Its significance? They used it to wash their hands and their brushes?"

"I suppose they did. They'd have to wash them somewhere, and it would be easier to go into the shed than to the bathroom or the laundry or the kitchen. But I wasn't thinking of that when I referred to the sink. If the theory of either of you is correct, why wasn't your murderer seen passing the kitchen window?"

"When you're in a kitchen you don't spend your time looking out of the window. Mrs Sayer wouldn't, anyway. She'd be busy at various places in the room."

"Hm, I suppose so. But Will could go out the back door into the shed without the risk of being seen by her. I suggest we change the subject. Who is your partner in the doubles this afternoon, George?"

* * *

Shortly after nine o'clock, Inspector Chambers called at the cottage. "I'm glad you haven't left yet."

"We have no matches today until two-thirty."

"Good. I think the time has come to inform the Harkin brothers of Cowan's accusation. I've been putting it off, but we're making no progress whatever. This murderer's too cunning to give himself away. All three of them have too much intelligence to fall into any of the verbal traps I set. Blast them. Well, this might rattle the confidence of the guilty one. Would you care to be present, Jabal? They've been told that you assist the police on occasion so it won't seem strange if you're with me."

"I'd prefer you to ask their permission. We've been on friendly terms."

"Right. We'll ask them. Come over to the house with me. I think it best to question them in their own surroundings. One of my men is hunting them up."

"You're no longer suspecting Bruce, then?"

"I incline to think it's Will or Casey we're after, but I certainly haven't eliminated Bruce. I'll tackle him when I go to the hospital. See how he reacts to the news."

Madeleine answered the door at the Harkins' house. The Inspector said, "I'd like to have a word with your brothers, Miss Harkin. I've asked them to come in, if it's convenient. I wonder if I could see them alone somewhere?"

Madeleine's eyes widened. "Why do

you want them? Has something else happened? It's not Bruce, is it? Is Bruce all right? When we rang the hospital this morning they told us he'd been shifted but they wouldn't say where."

"He's doing fine. He's been moved to a private hospital, Miss Harkin. At public expense, so don't worry about that. He'll be home again before long."

"Which hospital? I want to go and see him."

"I don't have the name with me at the moment. I can look it out later for you." Trevor did not add that the private hospital was one he had nominated himself and that Bruce had been sent there on his instructions to ensure that his family could not contact him. The mind of a senior police officer is not imbued with simple, child-like trust. It turns at the drop of a hat to matters such as poisoned grapes, throttling with a pillow, and slipping lethal potions into a bedside glass of orange juice.

234

Madeleine led them into the living room. "Will here do? You — you, don't want me too?"

"No, it's unnecessary to take up any of your time, Miss Harkin, and we shan't keep your brothers long."

Madeleine gave a worried, puzzled look at Jabal and then left them. A few minutes later Will and Casey came into the room.

"What's the matter? Is it Bruce?" asked Casey.

"Bruce is all right." Trevor explained again that he had been shifted because of shortage of beds in the public hospital and assured them that he would not be kept long.

"Have they X-rayed his hand? It wasn't broken, was it?"

"I don't have the results," said Trevor truthfully.

"Then what's the matter?" demanded Will. "Has someone else been hurt?" He looked at Jabal.

"No," said Jabal. "But Mr Chambers has something to say to you and has asked me to be present. Have you any objections? I shall go if you have."

"No, of course not. You stay. But what is it? What's happened now?"

"Sit down please," said the Inspector. When they were settled, he regarded each keenly before he spoke. "There's something we have not yet told you concerning the death of Graham Cowan and I consider the time has come when we should do so. You know that Mr Jarrett, Mr Freeth and Mr Cumbit were all present when Cowan died? What we have not told you earlier is that in his last few moments the dying man made a statement. Perhaps, Mr Jarrett, you would repeat what he said to you?"

"I asked Cowan who had stabbed him," said Jabal. "He was fully conscious, he understood my question and he replied 'It was Mad's brother'. Then he began to name one of you. His lips seemed to form a B, but he did not have time to finish the word."

Both brothers were staring at him. Then they looked at each other, at the

Inspector and back to Jabal. Finally Will said, "He said that? Really?"

"It was quite clear. We all heard him. We made no mistake."

"And you've known all along, Jabal?" There was reproach in Will's voice.

The Inspector said, "It was at my request that Mr Jarrett did not repeat what he had heard."

There was a long silence. Then Chambers asked, "Have you anything to say? Either of you?"

Again the two brothers looked at each other. Then Will shook his head silently and Casey grunted, "No."

The Inspector went on, "We understand that Cowan was stabbed in a fit of anger. It was not a premeditated murder, and the charge will probably be reduced to manslaughter. The attack on your brother Bruce was fortunately unsuccessful and it is not inevitable that a charge of attempted murder will be added to the manslaughter charge. We have no proof that Bruce was deliberately hit with intent to kill. If we can establish the facts concerning the death of Cowan, the case can then be closed. I can't promise that, of course. The decision won't rest with me. But I am reasonably sure that only the one charge will be brought. Have I made myself clear?"

"Perfectly," said Will. Casey merely nodded.

"Now have you anything to tell me?"

Neither spoke.

"I shall be here all day and readily available if you decide to make a statement."

Trevor rose. Jabal looked searchingly at the faces of the two brothers but could read nothing from their expression. He did not speak himself. He got up and followed Trevor out of the room.

"You weren't long," said Madeleine, coming out of the kitchen when she heard them. "Can I ask what it's all about?"

"You can ask your brothers," said the Inspector.

Jabal hesitated. She was about to have a shock, if they told her but she may already know which one was the killer and would now be better able to persuade him to confess. "We have no golf matches this morning," he told her. "I'll be in the cottage all morning. If there's any way in which I can help in — er — in anything, don't hesitate to let me know." Then he left with Trevor.

"Did you notice any reaction of guilt?" asked the Inspector when they were outside the house.

"No. It was impossible to tell how the announcement affected them. There was obvious surprise, perhaps even amazement, to learn that Cowan had accused them, but that was a predictable reaction on the part of both the guilty one and the innocent. It told us nothing."

"Well, we'll hope something comes of it. Whichever one it is, he must now realise that he can't get away with it. The other may force him to tell."

"Yes." Jabal had a vision of Casey taking Will by the throat and shaking him wildly. "I hope you've done the right thing, Trevor."

"I'm not sure myself, but we were making no progress at all. It may bring results."

Trevor went over to the police caravan and Jabal walked slowly back to the cottage. The expression on the brothers' faces had been hard to interpret. Surprise had been there, but what else? Trevor had been right. It had been time to tell them. They were neither of them dull and must know that only the truth could put an end to the suffering of their family.

"What happened?" asked Alan. "Did either of them confess?"

"No, but it gave them something to think about."

"Why didn't the police tell them before?"

"Because it could have brought about false accusations, elaborate attempts to clear themselves and possibly attacks

240

one upon the other. Trevor's not sure now that he's acted wisely in telling them. As long as they didn't know they'd been accused by Cowan they were off their guard. Telling them was a last resort because no progress was being made by the detectives. It was risky. There could be unpleasant consequences and unnecessary complications. On the other hand, it may induce a confession. That's what Trevor's hoping — that the guilty one can no longer stand the strain of waiting."

Ten minutes later there was a knock at the door. It was Will Harkin, his face taut with worry. "Can I speak to you, Jabal? No, please don't go, you two. I'd prefer you all to be present and hear what I say. I have something to tell you."

"Sit down, Will."

Will sat, his hands clasped tightly together, his eyebrows pulled together in a frown. He first addressed Alan and George. "Jabal may have told you that

241

I now know what Cowan said before he died. We've been told. I wish I'd known sooner. I wouldn't have tried to get away with it. I just kept hoping the case would be dropped for lack of evidence." He turned to Jabal. "I'll go and see the Inspector but I wanted to tell you first. You've been so good and helpful to us in all this trouble."

There was silence. Then Jabal said gently, "Would you like to tell us how it happened?"

"I lost my temper," said Will. "It wasn't Cowan's fault. Don't think that. It was mine. I thought he had borrowed and snarled the fishing lines. I'd found them in the shed the day before, just when the tide was right for launching the boat. I know now that it wasn't Cowan. It was Clara. I should've suspected the cat in the first place. Of course I wouldn't have killed anyone just for tangling a few fishing lines. But when I accused Cowan he denied it and that angered me. One word led to another. There were other

242

matters on my mind which I won't bore you with just now. I had a few worries. No, I'm not making excuses. Cowan swore he hadn't touched the lines, and of course he hadn't, but I thought he was lying. I started abusing him and he quite naturally — quite understandably — retaliated. We started to row. Oh, I can't really say how it happened. I have a very bad temper. The knife was on the table. I took it up. I didn't intend to kill him. It was just the first thing I saw to use, to strike out with. I'll never forgive myself."

Alan and George looked at Jabal, waiting for him to comment, but he said nothing. He was looking earnestly at Will, and saw that the fingers were now unclasped and the frown had gone.

Alan was the first to speak. "The charge may be manslaughter," he said. "You've saved the rest of your family much trouble and worry. It was courageous of you to confess and it was the best thing to do."

"So Cowan was about to say 'Bill'?" asked George.

"Yes, of course," said Will. "Not many people call me that but he did. Well, I wanted you to know first. I shan't tell Madeleine. Others can do that when they've taken me away. It will save her an emotional scene. Perhaps she'll understand. Jabal, would you — that is if she . . . ?"

"I'll do anything I can," promised Jabal. "She's a sensible girl. But tell me — did you also attack Bruce?"

"Oh, Bruce? Yes — er — Bruce. I didn't want to kill Bruce. I thought he'd just jump. I don't want to talk about that. I had a good reason. I'll go over to see the Inspector now and make a full statement about Cowan." He got up and seemed much more composed than when he had come in. At the door he turned and said with dignity, "I want to thank you all, very sincerely, for all you've done and to apologise for the trouble and distress I've caused by not owning up before. Put it down to fear, cowardice, what you like." Then he turned abruptly and left.

"Poor fellow," remarked George. "Well, at least it's finished. He wasn't my pick. I thought it was Casey."

"I wonder why he hit Bruce," said Alan. "There seems no good reason for doing so."

"Bruce said he knew who'd killed Cowan. He must've seen Will going into the shed that afternoon."

"But Will admitted going several times into the shed to fetch tools. Perhaps he was wiping blood off his hands when he came out one time. Or if the door was open, Bruce might even have seen him actually commit the crime. What do you think, Jabal? You're not saying anything."

"I think it is a very stupid cat who'd choose to play with cords onto which are fastened large sharp fishhooks. In fact, I haven't seen Clara play at all. She is no longer a kitten."

"You think the argument started on some other account?"

"I don't think we can gain much by discussing it right now. Did you get a morning paper when you fetched the milk?"

It was some twenty minutes later that Inspector Chambers called. He came in and sank onto a kitchen chair. "Well, it's over."

"Yes, we know," Alan told him. "He came here first."

"Oh, did he? He didn't tell me that. He's confessed to the murder of Cowan but refuses to discuss Bruce's accident. Said he'd plead guilty to the murder and saw no reason to bring in the other incident. You know, if he hadn't made that attack on his young brother, I'd be inclined to feel sorry for the chap. It was the result of a sudden argument, as we thought, and his temper getting out of control."

"Yes, he told us," said Alan. "And over such a trivial matter to begin with."

"Oh, I don't know that I'd call it trivial. His whole business was at

246

stake. If a story like that got around it could ruin him. The public have been warned about those cars, but they still fall in."

"What cars?" asked George. "He didn't mention cars to us."

"Oh, didn't he tell you what caused the argument? He sold Cowan one of those cars that had been in the Invercargill floods. I didn't know any had come up as far as Auckland, but it seems he'd got hold of a few cheap. You must've read in the papers that they're allowed to be sold by dealers only on condition that the full facts are stated on the transfer title. You see, the parts can rust in a few months' time and give no end of trouble. Anyway, Cowan found out and accused him that afternoon in the shed. He says it was the very fact that he was in the wrong and that his garage had worked a swindle that made him lose his temper. He just picked up the knife on the table . . . "

"Trevor!" interrupted Jabal. "Hold

on a minute. Who are you talking about?"

"Why, Casey Harkin, of course. I thought you knew. He's just come and confessed."

14

"THEY weren't very clever stories, were they?" said Alan. "I've remembered I saw the fishing lines being put away once. They're kept in the shed, in a wooden chest with a lid, where Clara can't get at them. They wouldn't risk her getting a hook into one of her little paws. And Casey has said before that he hadn't met Cowan until he came here this summer and Bradley introduced him. How could he have sold him a car? Those Invercargill cars have been in the news lately so it gave him an idea."

"Since they both made false confessions," said George, "I assume the murderer is Bruce. Is that so, Jabal?"

"We can't assume both confessions were false. That's only one of several possibilities."

"You mean one of them was telling the truth?"

"I mean one of them may yet prove to be the murderer of Cowan. One who is guilty of a crime will sometimes confess to it in such a way that his statement is sure to be doubted, and then discounted as false. It's then assumed he is innocent. A not uncommon manoeuvre."

"If that's so, which one was it?"

"The one with the silliest story, I should say. If he wanted it to be seen through, he'd tell obvious lies."

"Ah — Will."

"No, no," said George. "It would be Casey."

"On the other hand," continued Jabal, "one confession may have been sincerely made, with no intent of guile, but a fictitious reason for the quarrel with Cowan substituted for the real one. That gives rise to thought — what was the actual cause of the disagreement? Why does the killer wish to conceal it? The other confession may have been made with the purpose of protecting a brother. If so, which? Why does one consider another to be guilty? Has he evidence he is reluctant to pass on to the police?"

"Must you complicate things like this, Jabal? I thought we'd got somewhere at last."

"We're no further ahead than we were. If both confessions were false, why was Bruce attacked? Did one decide to kill him because he was a murderer and they didn't think he should live to murder others? Or was it neither Will nor Casey who wanted Bruce to fall? Is the incident quite unrelated to the stabbing of Cowan?"

"Oh, don't! My head's whirling," groaned Alan.

"My own head's whirling, too," Jabal told him. "It's a maelstrom of inconsistencies, improbabilities, and facts that don't accord."

"I suggest," said George mildly, "that we drop the subject at least until after lunch. We could go outside and practise putting until then."

"An excellent idea," said Alan. "Our heads may clear a little."

"Yes, indeed," agreed Jabal. "That's a good suggestion, George. I mustn't go away from the cottage, but we could use that flat patch in front, and do some chip shots, too. But I wonder . . . why did both Will and Casey refuse to discuss Bruce's accident? Do you think that was because . . . ?"

"Stop it," ordered Alan. "This minute!"

The morning passed without further incident, and, through the initial efforts of George and Alan, without further discussion of the Harkins' problem. A natural hollow in the sand in front of the cottage provided an excellent substitute for a bunker, and the manipulation of a number eight soon preoccupied their thoughts. A bathe before lunch completed the relaxation. At twelve-thirty they sat down to a meal of bread, tomatoes, and boiled eggs.

The conversation continued to centre

on the difficulties of successful handling of a wedge and the advisability of avoiding such difficulties by the simple means of skirting round the bunkers lurking on the treacherous number four hole.

It was nearly half-past one when Madeleine knocked at the back door.

"I suppose it's too late for your lunch," she said, "but perhaps you can use them for your tea tonight."

"Bless you, my dear," said George, as he took the dish from her. "You have some angelic qualities. Date again, I see."

"Of course, Mr Cumbit. I wouldn't consider any other sort."

"How has your morning been?" asked Jabal, wondering if she knew of her brothers' confessions.

"Not very pleasant. Everyone is in a grumpy mood, including me. The Inspector came over early this morning and spoke to Case and Will but he didn't tell me what it was about and they didn't either. Then before lunch he came again, looking daggers and asked me to fetch them both. I don't understand what's going on. He asked me quite politely if he could use the living room again if it was unoccupied but then when the boys arrived he positively glowered at them and ordered them into the room. I just heard something like 'wasting my time and hindering proceedings' and then he shut the door. What was he talking about? After a few minutes he came out still scowling and went straight out the back door without even speaking to me. Then Boxer and Will came out and they were cross too. One said 'You blithering ass' and at the same time the other was saying 'You crazy fool' and they glared at each other. Then one of them laughed and said, 'Oh, come on, we'll fix that carburettor' and they went into the garage together to work on Will's car."

"Where are they now?"

"We're all still at lunch, except Brad. He's just gone off to take a phone message to someone in a bach up the hill, but he'll be back soon. I'm brewing fresh coffee and thought I'd bring these over while I'm waiting for it to percolate."

"And you're grumpy?" said Alan. "You hide it very well."

"We all are. I'm peeved because something's going on and no one will tell me what it is or why the Inspector called. Roma's worried because more Lodge guests checked out. I think the Lodge is empty now. It's not Roma's fault and it shouldn't worry her, but it does. And Irma's sunburned. She forgot to put cream on her nose this morning and it's all red and going to peel and she hates not being neat and unblemished. Will and Boxer aren't snarling at each other any more but they're quiet and sulky and won't talk, as though they're brooding over something."

"Perhaps Casey is still suffering from his flea bites," suggested Alan. "Most distressing for him."

"What flea bites?"

"You told us yesterday that he'd got fleas from Clara and that had helped to put him in a bad mood."

Madeleine stared. "Clara doesn't have fleas. At least if she does she doesn't give them to us. I didn't say that."

"You did, my dear," said Alan. "You said it distinctly."

"You must have misheard or else I'm going crazy. What exactly did I say?"

Jabal answered her. "You were telling us that Casey was going to search the Lodge for that knife Bruce saw come down on his fingers, and that he was very angry. You said he'd picked up fleas from the cat and was, understandably, in a really bad temper. It's of no consequence. We just wondered if they were still irritating him."

"But I said no such thing," protested Madeleine. "I'm sure I didn't. I don't know what you're talking about. Surely I haven't gone completely off my head? 'Picked up fleas from the cat'? Of course I didn't say that. Oh! *Oh!*" She began to laugh. "Oh, I see. I'm awfully sorry. I know what must've happened. I do that at times when I'm upset. Not *fleas* from the *cat*. He'd picked up *keys* from the *flat*."

They laughed with her. "We'd imagined him bathing in disinfectant," said Alan, "and getting you to wash all his clothes."

"Our apologies to Clara," said Jabal. "It's easy to do that when you have other things on your mind. I remember one morning I provoked unsuppressed giggles in my congregation by expressing a devout wish that they might all be visited by the geese of Pod."

"Did you? I'm glad other people do it too. I'd better get back now. That coffee will be ready."

"Poor girl," said George when she had left. "Her brothers can't have told her that they confessed. How kind of her to think of us at such a time and bring more scones. Would you like one now, Alan, or shall we keep them for tea? What about you, Jabal?"

Jabal looked blankly at him. "Fleas," he murmured, "fleas from the cat."

"Well, the poor girl was upset."

"Of course she was," said Jabal. "What a fool I've been! What an utter fool!"

"What's the matter?"

"I must see them. Come over with me, will you? Straight away, while they're all there together." He was already going out the back door.

George and Alan followed him, in slight bewilderment, to the Harkins' kitchen. Madeleine had the coffee pot in her hand, about to take it into the dining room.

"Are your family still at the table?" asked Jabal bluntly. "May we come in? I'd like a word with them."

"Of course. Come and have some coffee with us." She showed them into the dining room where Irma, Roma, Will and Casey were seated at the table.

Will got to his feet. "Oh, come in.

How nice to see you." He pulled forward some chairs. "Sit down. You'll have coffee, won't you? Mad's just made it."

"No, thank you," said Jabal and remained standing. He looked round the table at each of them in turn and then said, "Mrs Sayer, would you care to tell us why you stabbed Graham Cowan?"

No one spoke. Jabal heard a faint gasp from Madeleine who was at his side. The others stared at him briefly, then all eyes turned to Irma Sayer. She had been taken aback at the unexpected question. Now she flushed with anger. "What are you talking about? How dare you come in here and say a thing like that to me?"

"It was you who killed Cowan," repeated Jabal calmly.

She rose, indignant. "You silly old fool! What gives you the right to throw an accusation like that at me? I'll have you for slander."

"I don't think so, Mrs Sayer. There

is too much evidence against you. Did you also injure Bruce's fingers with a knife handle, in order to make him fall down the cliff?"

"What evidence?" She was still standing and now her hands were clenched.

"The blow which killed Cowan was a left-handed one. You are the only truly left-handed person here."

"That's nothing. Anyone could have used a left hand."

"The blow on Bruce's hand was also made by a left-handed person, one wearing a gold ring. You wear a wedding ring."

"Dozens of people wear rings."

"Your thumb print was on the blade of the knife that killed Cowan."

"Well, I know that, you stupid fool. The Inspector told me. I'd been cleaning fish with it earlier on."

"You were in the kitchen that afternoon, the nearest place to the shed, and had the best opportunity to go into it without being seen."

"That doesn't prove I did. This is raving nonsense."

"And above all, Graham Cowan, before he died, had time to tell us that you were the one who stabbed him."

She stared and for the first time her voice wavered. "He — he told you that?"

"Mr Freeth, Mr Cumbit and I were all there and heard clearly what he said. We are, I think, considered reputable witnesses and our word will not be doubted in a court of law."

"He *told* you?" she repeated, as if dazed by the shock. "Why was I not informed before?"

They were all looking at her with various expressions of dismay and astonishment. Jabal said, "The police wanted to establish motive first. They were also allowing time for the killer to confess."

"I'm going to my room." She walked unsteadily to the door, past Jabal, and they heard her footsteps going up the stairs.

There was silence in the dining room, broken at last by George Cumbit, who turned in disapproval to Jabal and said, "But you tricked her. You lied."

"I did not lie."

"You said Cowan told us she stabbed him."

"No. I said he had time to tell us, and I said we heard clearly what he said. Remember Madeleine's spoonerism — 'fleas from the cat'? As you pointed out, she was upset. But being stabbed to death is also, we must presume, a disturbing experience. What Cowan *said* was 'Mad's brother'. What he *meant* to say was 'Brad's mother'. Unlike Madeleine, he instantly realised his mistake and tried to correct it. 'I mean' he began, then his strength failed him." He turned to the Harkins. "We'll leave you now. You will have much to discuss together."

Roma, Will and Casey were still speechless as Madeleine showed the three men out. She started to walk with them over to the cottage and suddenly all the pent-up questions and exclamations seemed to bubble out of her at once. "Is it true? Can you prove it? The boys didn't do it? None of them? Will Bruce come home now? How did you know? What will happen? Will Irma . . . ?"

Jabal stopped, turned to her and interrupted the flow of words. "I think you'd better go back, my child. Bradley will be home soon and he is going to need you."

"Oh, yes, of course. Oh, my poor, poor Brad!" She turned and ran.

15

"SHE'S signed a statement," said Jabal that evening, "and they've taken her in to Auckland. The police caravan will be removed tomorrow, Trevor says, when a few loose ends have been tied and formalities completed."

"Thank God it's over. I'm sorry for Bradley."

"Yes, but he has Madeleine to console him and he's marrying into a good family. They stuck together through this affair and they'll stick by him in his coming ordeal. They're a fine, loyal lot."

"That's not the way you described them at first," remarked Alan. "You suspected each of the brothers."

"Of course. I was convinced that one of them was the killer, yet everything *except* Cowan's statement indicated otherwise. I twisted all the evidence to fit a theory that was erroneous in the first place. As fast as you two pointed out discrepancies, I brushed them aside. I should have known better."

"Don't blame yourself. How *could* you have known?"

"For one thing, Madeleine told us that Cowan never called her 'Mad'. I talked myself into believing that he would do so in that one instance. It was so much shorter, I said. So it is, but when you're used to calling a person, and thinking of a person, by one name, you do not, even in a moment of stress, or perhaps especially in a moment of stress, refer to that person by an unfamiliar nickname."

"I suppose not."

"'Brad' is the common abbreviation for Bradley. They all call him that. Graham was Bradley's friend and Mrs Sayer was predominantly 'Brad's mother' to him. That's the way he thought of her."

"Well, he thought of the Harkins as

Madeleine's brothers."

"That's true, but one of you asked why he didn't just say 'Bill' or 'Bruce'. To state first that it was Madeleine's brother is understandable, but why say 'I mean'? It would be more natural, as you remarked at the time, simply to add the name. 'I mean' is a customary preface to the correction of an error. Cowan knew he'd muddled his consonants and tried again. 'I mean' he began. Then he died."

"You couldn't be expected to reason that out."

"Perhaps not, but there were so may other facts pointing to Irma Sayer as the killer. She's the only one who is fully left-handed. She was in the best position to slip into the shed and kill Cowan. The window of the kitchen looks on to the shed and the family must have known she was working in the kitchen. It would be a stupid risk for any other would-be murderer to take. He would surely wait for a more suitable occasion. She was also in the best position — the only position — to attack Bruce without the risk of being seen. She told us, and the police verified her statement, that from where she fishes she could not see any of the others until Casey once swam out beyond the surf. So obviously they could not see her. She could climb up without fear of being noticed. For anyone else to have done so would be a foolhardy risk, too rash even for a determined killer."

"That's right. There were people climbing up from the front, a couple of bathers on the left, and Casey, Will and Bradley to the right."

"And Roma part-way round the base. But Mrs Sayer had a passage up from the seaface of the Lion and we were told she often went that way when caught by the tide. She was well used to the climb, she knew the time Bruce would start and the route he would take. She could be in position, waiting for him. All the others would've been pressed for time to get up there before he did.

Moreover, she, Casey and Madeleine are the only ones of the household who wear a ring."

"She seemed genuinely shocked at Bruce's accident."

"She was. She was shocked and disappointed that her attempt to get rid of him had failed. She couldn't see what happened from where she was. She could only just reach his fingers with her knife handle. His left hand let go at once under her blows, his right, he told us, was in a niche, protected by rock projections. She assumed he would drop and she scrambled hastily back to her fishing spot."

"What a good thing we were watching."

"She knew we intended to do so. We would be convenient witnesses to the supposed accident, as we were too far below to see the top of his fingers or the knife descend on them."

"What about those 'significant facts' you gave us, Jabal? Wait a minute. I have the paper here. First — Bruce told us he'd go straight to the police if he had any evidence or proof to offer."

"He also told us he would do anything to save his brothers and Bradley, so the person he suspected could not have been one of them. He was devoted to Madeleine, too. He wouldn't have informed on any of them. That pointed to Mrs Sayer or Roma as the object of his suspicions."

"Well, your second point — Mrs Sayer is a very keen fisherwoman."

"I do not fish myself," said Jabal, "but even I know that one essential of a line fisherman's equipment is a strong knife. Only a fairly small black-handled knife belonging to the Harkins was found in Mrs Sayer's kit. Yet she hoped for big game and she had brought her own gear. Where was her knife? She borrowed one that morning because she had a more brutal use in mind for her own, which she would then discard in the sea. She needed one with a large, heavy handle. Apart from the one used to stab Cowan and now in the hands of the police, those in the Harkin shed were not big enough for her purpose. She had to sacrifice her own."

"But none of the Harkins recognised Bruce's description of the knife. Wouldn't they have seen it in her kit?"

"How could they? She fished alone and she complained to us that they never invited her out in the boat with them. Her son Bradley may have seen it. If so, he must've had some sleepless nights. Perhaps he'll tell us later."

"Well, I can't see what your third 'significant fact' has to do with it all," said Alan. "A sink in the shed?"

"I told you that the personalities of those involved are always important. Mrs Sayer was meticulously clean and tidy. She wouldn't let Madeleine leave one unwashed dish or spoon on the bench overnight. Can you imagine her cleaning fish that morning and not then thoroughly washing and wiping the knife? There was a sink available. When one has just wiped a knife, it is usual to pick it up by the handle, avoiding the blade, and replace it in position. We all do that when we wipe the dishes. Yet Mrs Sayer's standard of cleanliness is higher than ours. She is most unlikely to have touched the blade and left a thumb print as she put it back on the table. But when you pick up a knife in order to use it — hand me that bread knife, will you, George?"

"What for?" George reached for the bread-knife and handed it over.

"Did you see how he picked it up, Alan? It was not only the handle that his fingers touched."

"But I turned it round to offer you the handle."

"Take it up, Alan, and stab that scone with it. Don't think. Just do it. See? You touched the blade in order to change your grip. That would be the case with any large knife. Mrs Sayer fingered the blade as well as the handle when she lifted the knife off the table to stab Cowan. She wiped her prints

271

off the handle and didn't think of the blade. Trevor tells me that car thieves are caught by fingerprints on the roof of the car, desk robbers by prints on top of the desk, not on the drawer they've rifled. They unconsciously place the hand they're not using on some nearby object."

"Why did she do it, Jabe? She had nothing to fear from Cowan."

"No, but Bradley had. Cowan was threatening him, and she must have known."

"That seems a poor motive for her killing him."

"On the contrary, it was a very strong motive. There are few urges more powerful than that of a mother to protect her son."

"I admired that woman. She seemed honest and truthful."

"Yes, she is. She was truthful when she told us she knew who had killed Cowan. It amused her to do so. She was confident that we would never discover the truth. Confident and satisfied, at that stage, even happy, I think. The desire accomplished is sweet to the soul."

"It's hard to forgive the attack on Bruce."

"It's hard to forgive either attack, as both were planned. We assumed that Cowan was killed in a fit of rage but I doubt if that was the case. I think she went out to the shed with the specific object of killing him. She knew the knife was there — she'd used it that morning and replaced it. She was strong and determined. He would not turn his back and she had little time — Will might come out at any moment for another tool — so she let him have it face on. A dangerous woman."

"More coffee?" asked George. "Hand your cups."

"At least the family are now freed from suspicion," said Alan. "I feel I'll be able to concentrate on my golf a little better now. I had unusual difficulty this afternoon in driving off the tee."

"You can't blame the Harkins' problems for that," said George, "especially as Jabal had told us the killer before we left for golf. You are merely offering an excuse for bad play. You tee your ball too low."

"I had trouble too at the first few tees," said Jabal. "But I think I tend to grip too tightly."

"Perhaps you bend over too far at the address. Where's that book of Will's?"

"If you don't grip tightly, you're liable to shift the clubface from its proper position at the top of the swing."

"That's what I do," said George. "A chap out there today said a good tip is to keep the little finger of the left hand from being loosened, then the next two automatically stay firm."

"My fault today was the position of my left arm. It's not easy to whip your right hand into the shot when you're concentrating on keeping your left elbow straight."

"That's true. And if you fail to cock

your wrists in the proper horizontal plane . . . "

The sun was sinking below the horizon at Piha Beach. The sparrows had chirped their goodnight chorus in the acacia trees, the sea was changing colour from indigo and gold to a deep silver grey, and the lengthening shadow of the Rock Lion was beginning to merge softly with the colour of the dark iron sands, as in Canna Cottage three reverend gentlemen settled down, over a borrowed book, a pot of coffee and a plate of date scones, to discuss some of the vexatious problems that beset the human race.

THE END

A FOOT IN THE GRAVE
Bruce Marshall

About to be imprisoned and tortured in Buenos Aires, John Smith escapes, only to become involved in an aeroplane hijacking.

DEAD TROUBLE
Martin Carroll

Trespassing brought Jennifer Denning more than she bargained for. She was totally unprepared for the violence which was to lie in her path.

HOURS TO KILL
Ursula Curtiss

Margaret went to New Mexico to look after her sick sister's rented house and felt a sharp edge of fear when the absent landlady arrived.

THE DEATH OF ABBE DIDIER
Richard Grayson

Inspector Gautier of the Sûreté investigates three crimes which are strangely connected.

NIGHTMARE TIME
Hugh Pentecost

Have the missing major and his wife met with foul play somewhere in the Beaumont Hotel, or is their disappearance a carefully planned step in an act of treason?

BLOOD WILL OUT
Margaret Carr

Why was the manor house so oddly familiar to Elinor Howard? Who would have guessed that a Sunday School outing could lead to murder?

THE DRACULA MURDERS
Philip Daniels

The Horror Ball was interrupted by a spectral figure who warned the merrymakers they were tampering with the unknown.

THE LADIES OF LAMBTON GREEN
Liza Shepherd

Why did murdered Robin Colquhoun's picture pose such a threat to the ladies of Lambton Green?

CARNABY AND THE GAOLBREAKERS
Peter N. Walker

Detective Sergeant James Aloysius Carnaby-King is sent to prison as bait. When he joins in an escape he is thrown headfirst into a vicious murder hunt.

MUD IN HIS EYE
Gerald Hammond

The harbourmaster's body is found mangled beneath Major Smyle's yacht. What is the sinister significance of the illicit oysters?

THE SCAVENGERS
Bill Knox

Among the masses of struggling fish in the *Tecta*'s nets was a larger, darker, ominously motionless form . . . the body of a skin diver.

DEATH IN ARCADY
Stella Phillips

Detective Inspector Matthew Furnival works unofficially with the local police when a brutal murder takes place in a caravan camp.

STORM CENTRE
Douglas Clark

Detective Chief Superintendent Masters, temporarily lecturing in a police staff college, finds there's more to the job than a few weeks relaxation in a rural setting.

THE MANUSCRIPT MURDERS
Roy Harley Lewis

Antiquarian bookseller Matthew Coll, acquires a rare 16th century manuscript. But when the Dutch professor who had discovered the journal is murdered, Coll begins to doubt its authenticity.

SHARENDEL
Margaret Carr

Ruth didn't want all that money. And she didn't want Aunt Cass to die. But at Sharendel things looked different. She began to wonder if she had a split personality.

MURDER TO BURN
Laurie Mantell

Sergeants Steven A_____ and I___
Brendon, of the N_____
force, come upo_____
in the water. Whe_____
is identified the_____
that they are inve_____
fraud.

YOU CAN___
Maisie B_____

Whilst running t_____
Bureau, Kate We_____
with no apparent_____
body of one of her clients is found
in her room.

DAGGERS DRAWN
Margaret Carr

Stacey Manston was the kind of
girl who could take most things in
her stride, but three murders were
something different . . .